AM

Cross My Heart

Anjel

http://www.pilotgrouppub.com

PILOT PUBLISHING

Pilot Publishing Group
9122 Mackerel Drive
Texas City, Texas 77591

ISBN 0-9761025-2-8

First Printing July 2007
Printed in United States of America

Cover Artist: Marion Designs
Typesetter: D. Williams

Dedicated to…

My Family…..

My parents, my two sisters and brother, my Man

My girls….

My Rock, my TBAM, the nuttiest Dominican I know,

and the two "freest" chicks I know

I LOVE YOU ALL

And Supastar, thanks for giving me my chance to shine

PILOT PUBLISHING

PART ONE:

OLD FRIENDS

PILOT PUBLISHING

CHAPTER 1

Kia

I sighed as we ran through the song for maybe the tenth time. I don't know what it was, but my voice just wasn't working for some reason. I fucked up on the fourth line and groaned as I made a gesture across my neck signaling to my producer to cut off the track.

"Aight, Kia," I heard my producer, Tyrone, say through the headphones, "come on out the booth. We'll take a break. You can get some tea or just somethin' to wet your throat. Get your head right, and we'll start again in twenty minutes."

I nodded as I placed the headset back on the stand and opened the door to walk out. I bent down to straighten the laces on my black Manolos and noticed Tyrone starin' at my ass in my jean mini. I couldn't really blame him, shit, I was a full-fledged, chocolate-skinned, black female with hurt me curves and long brown hair. (Actually, it's a weave, but you can't tell by lookin', I got the good shit.) I stood up and smiled at him to let 'im know that I'd caught him. He just smiled back and turned toward one of the engineers in the room. I knew that man wanted me, but I was not havin' it. That business-wit'-pleasure shit never worked.

I walked out of the studio and down the hall to the caf. It was a Sunday, so not many heads were in the buildin'. I got some change out of my purse as I walked over to the vending machines. I bought myself a Vanilla Coke and a bag of Doritos, 'cuz lord knew I was starving. Then I sat down to eat.

As I thought about why I, Kia Haughton—dancer/singer/songwriter—was not hitting my notes that day in the studio, I couldn't help but be happy with what I had accomplished in my short twenty-one years on this earth. I lived in LA—born and raised in a town full of wannabe stars—and although I did have to place myself in that category, I was now working at a small, up-and-coming record label as a backup singer. And I was working on my demo so that I can get signed.

When I was finished with my snack I got up and threw the empty chip bag away, and brought my half-full soda with me. And that was when I saw him comin' straight down the hall in the other direction—brown eyes, medium-toned skin, baggy jeans, and braids. And he was tall, really tall. He had always towered over my short self.

David

"I think we're in the wrong building," I told my boy Kareem as we circled the hall for maybe the tenth time.

"No," he said. "We're in the right building. We just gotta find the right studio. . . ." He trailed off as his gaze moved down the hall.

I followed it and noticed this beautiful, brown-skinned sista comin' up to us. She had long, brown hair and an hourglass figure. You could see how shapely and firm her legs were in the mini skirt she wore.

"Maybe she can help us find our way," Kareem said with a smile as he patted my arm.

The sista came right up to us and smiled at me. It was a pretty smile with perfectly even, white teeth, and a dimple on her right cheek. She looked like she was waiting for me to speak.

"Don't just stand there," she said. "Gimme a hug, boy."

She opened her arms and I looked back at her in confusion.

"I'm sorry, sweetheart, do I know you?" Her arms dropped to her sides.

"David, are you serious? You don't recognize me?" I shook my head.

"I'm sorry, but I don't. And I feel bad, too. You'd think I would remember someone as fine as you." She blushed and giggled a little. Then it clicked and I looked into her eyes more closely. "Chunky?" I asked. She held up a finger.

"Uh-uh." She spun around. "Not so much anymore."

I checked her out again and agreed.

"You look good," I told her and then I actually did pull her in for a warm hug.

Kia "Chunky" Haughton. We'd grown up together, well, sort of. Our mothers were best friends. They went to school together in Brooklyn, where I'm from. When Kia's mom was pregnant and engaged, she moved across the nation to Cali. But our moms kept in constant contact, still do, and as a result, Kia and I saw a lot of each other growin' up. We took bathes together when were little and the whole nine. I got pictures. Every summer one of us was traveling with our mothers to the opposite end of the U.S. But she was chubby back then, really chubby, hence the nickname. She was like the little sister I never had, *but lil' sis is all grown up now*, I thought to myself.

"I haven't seen you since you left New York. How are you?" I asked Kia.

"Good, good," she said. Kareem then cleared his throat and nudged me, making her glance his way with a grin. "Aren'tchu gonna introduce me to your friend?" she asked.

"Oh," I said with a smile. "This is my girl, Kia Haughton. Kia, Kareem, my best friend and manager."

"Manager?" she asked in a confused tone. "Are you the rapper that they wanted me to meet today?" I nodded my head slowly.

"You're the singer?" She nodded too.

"What happened to school?"

"Oh, I graduated with honors." I grinned as I proudly placed my hand on chest. "You're lookin' at a qualified physical therapist now."

"Really? Go 'head, boy." I nodded again.

"Yeah, butchu know I only went to school to satisfy my mother. I figured I'd take a year off and try to do somethin' for me." I had gone straight from high school through college, and now that I was twenty-three and done everything my mother asked of me, I wanted to try my hand at my true passion.

"I hear you. I knew you rapped, but I never thought we'd actually get to work with one another. This world is too small."

"Tell me about it," I said in agreement. She looked at her watch.

"We'd better head to the studio then. My producer is probably havin' a coronary by now."

We all laughed and she led the way. After our session, we headed out to the parking lot.

"So, where you stayin'?" she asked me as we reached our cars.

"The Marriott, downtown," I told her.

Her nose crinkled in disapproval and she shook her head.

"A hotel? You should just stay with me." I smiled.

"I appreciate the offer," I said, "but I don't wanna put you out. I really don't know how long I'm stayin'."

"Oh please, boy," she said with a wave of her hand. "You're not puttin' me out. I got plenty of room at my place." She smiled at Kareem. "Your boy can even stay. And it's the least I can do after whatchu did for me in New York."

While Kia was workin' as a dancer in New York a couple years ago, I let her stay wit' me. She was my roommate for two years before she went back home.

"Besides," she said with another smile, "my mother would kill me if she knew you were in town and I didn't offer you a place to stay." I chuckled.

"True."

She unlocked her silver Acura and reached inside. She took out a pen and ripped a scrap of paper out of one of her notebooks. She pressed on my back as she wrote.

"Here is my house number and my cell. Call me and lemme know whatchu wanna do. OK?"

I nodded and she hopped into her car. She started it up and rolled down the windows.

"See ya lata," she said as she squinted up at me, the sun in her eyes. She grinned at my boy and winked. "Bye, Kareem." He smiled.

"Bye."

With that, she sped off. Kareem unlocked the door to his black Navigator and we hopped in.

"So you've gotta tell me how you know this girl," Kareem said as he started the car up and drove off.

"Our moms are best friends."

"So y'all like grew up together?" I nodded. He grinned. "You ever hit that, son?" he asked and I laughed.

"No."

"Why not? That girl is a dime, man." I silently agreed.

"I never thought of her like that, dawg. She's like my sister." I smiled. "Besides she was kinda thick as a teenager." He raised his eyebrows.

"How thick?"

"*Real* thick. Her nickname was 'Chunky' when we were little."

"Really?" he asked in surprise. I nodded. "You would never know it to look at her now."

"Word." Kareem thought for a second.

"But I'm sayin', though," he started, "if you only think of her as a sister, then you can hook a *brotha* up." I laughed again.

"Aight, dawg. I'll put in a good word for you," I told him as he hit the interstate, but I silently thought, *he will never be able to handle Kia.* That girl was and would always be a pimp.

Kia

"Momma?!" I yelled as I walked into her house through the backdoor.

"I'll be down in a second, baby!" she called back in her east-coast accent.

"Who dat?! Chunky?!" I heard my big sister Liyah, call out. She was three years older than me.

"Yeah, girl," I answered as I walked down to my mother's finished basement.

She smiled and hugged me when I got down there. She was watching TV.

"What's good?" I asked.

"Nothin'," she replied. "I just stopped by for a quick visit. Gotta be at work soon."

I sat down on the couch next to her.

"It's nice and cool down here. It's hot as a mothafucka outside."

"I know, right? I can't wait until this heat wave is over."

"You and me both, girl."

"So tell me," Liyah said as she poked me in the side with her elbow, "who is this new guy I saw you wit' the otha day?"

I smiled.

"His name is Desire."

"Fits him 'cuz that man was fine."

"Word, but he could *not* work it in the bedroom."

"Seriously?" I nodded.

"Good sex is so hard to find," I said with a laugh and Liyah laughed with me, then she looked at her watch.

"Oh, shit, I gotta go." We hugged again. "But I will see you later."

"OK, bye."

She walked up the stairs and I pulled out one of the family albums. I flipped it open as I sat back. I smiled. There were pictures of me and David in the bathtub. We bathed together until we were about four and five. Our mothers

thought it time to stop when we learned to differentiate between male and female. I laughed to myself thinkin' about it.

I turned the page and smiled again. It was a picture of
David and me on my fifteenth birthday.

I sat back and reflected for a moment. That was also
the night of my first real date. It was with Dean Sanders. He
was eighteen and one of the finest dudes on our varsity foot-
ball team. I'd had a crush on him for a while and was so excited when he told me he wanted to take me out for my birthday. I was also so nervous that I'd switched my outfit for
about the fifth time when I heard a knock on my bedroom
door.

"Come in," I called through the door.

David stepped in with a smile. He looked me over. I
had combed out my wrap and bumped the edges. I had on a
knee length jean skirt and a blue long-sleeved top with high-
heeled Mary-Janes that I was workin' even in all my thick-
ness. "You look pretty," he told me. I smiled as put on some
hoop earrings.

"Thank you."

He leaned against the doorframe. "Where y'all goin'
tonight?" he asked. I grinned.

"Not sure. He said he wanted to surprise me."

"You really like this dude, huh."

"Am I that obvious?" He chuckled.

"Kinda." His expression changed to a serious one.
"Just make sure this dude keeps his hands to himself." I giggled.

"Aww, didn't know you cared so much," I teased. He
smiled.

"Just make sure. 'Cuz if he tries anything, he's gonna
get dealt with." I smiled again. "And promise me you won't
fall for any corny lines or games." I giggled again.

"You really ain't givin' me any credit." His expression turned serious again.

"I'm serious, Chunky," he said. I will never forget the
concern and sincerity I saw in his brown eyes that night. I
nodded.

"OK, David, I promise. Cross my heart," I told him with a smile as I made the gesture across my chest.

My mother came down then, interrupting my thoughts, and we kissed cheeks.

"Hey, sweetie," she said as she sat down next to me. "Takin' a walk down memory lane, huh?" I nodded as I flipped another page. "You know, David's in town." I smiled.

"You're too little too late, Ma," I said. "I bumped into him earlier."

"Oh really? Where?" I looked at her.

"The studio. Turns out we'll be working together."

"Well, isn't that nice. It's about time." I didn't respond, just smiled again. "You did offer him a place to stay while he's in town, right?" I laughed.

"Of course."

"Oh, aren't you two cute," she said as she looked at a picture of us in the pool. "You know, me and Pam always thought you two would end up together." Pam was David's mother.

I looked at her.

"That would never happen."

"Why you say that?" she asked curiously. I looked away from her.

"'Cuz he's not attracted to me."

"Did he tell you that?" I shook my head.

"It was obvious. David Green wouldn't be caught dead with the fat girl."

My mother took my chin in her hands and turned my face to look at her.

"You're beautiful now and you were just as beautiful then."

"Yeah, I know, Ma, but not everybody thinks the same way we do." She shook her head.

"I think you need to give that boy a little more credit. I thought he had a crush on you when you guys were in high school."

"If he did, he never said a thing to me. He wouldn't have admitted it even if he had."

"Well, if weight was the only thing holding him back, he has no excuse now, right?" I nodded and then smiled.

"He did tell me that I was fine today." She smiled back.

"Yeah?" I nodded again.

"He didn't recognize me at first."

"See? Don't sell yourself short, baby. I've always told you that."

"I think that advice is the reason I was never lacking in boyfriends."

She nodded in agreement and stood up.

"Come on. We can finish this conversation upstairs while you help me cook dinner."

Knock, knock, knock!

I ran downstairs to the front door of my condo and opened it. David and Kareem were standing there with suitcases in their hands.

"Hey, y'all," I greeted them with a big smile. David had decided to stay with me while he was in California, and today he was moving in. Kareem was going to keep his hotel room, though. "Damn," I said as I let them in and looked at all the luggage in their hands, "how long were you planning on staying again?" David laughed.

"Told you I wasn't sure."

"Obviously. Come on," I said as I gestured inside. "I'll give you the grand tour and show you to your room." I held my arms open. "This is the living room." I walked toward the kitchen and they followed. "This is the kitchen." I pointed down a small hallway. "The den is back there with a computer and another TV. There's also another bedroom. Sometimes Liyah or my girl Karen likes to stay the night, and that's where they stay." I walked upstairs and they followed. I gestured at the first bedroom. "This is my bedroom." I walked farther up the hall. "This will be your bathroom," I told David. "The washer and dryer are right here across the hall, and"—I opened up the last door at the end of the hall, blue comforter and curtains,—"this is your room. You can change the covers and stuff if you don't like 'em."

"Damn, girl," Kareem said. "This ain't a condo. It's a mansion." I giggled.

"Yeah, Kia," David agreed as they set down the suitcases, "this is far from my apartment in Brooklyn." I smiled.

"Told you I had plenty of room, didn't I?"

Knock, knock!

"Oh," I said, "that must be Karen. Y'all make yourselves at home. I'll be right back."

I ran downstairs and opened the front door.

"Wassup, girl?" she said as I let her in. "Whose Maxima is that next to your car?"

"Oh, that's my boy, David. He's gonna be stayin' wit' me for a little while. Come on in and I'll introduce you." We both ran upstairs and into David's room.

"Hey, guys," I said. "I wanna introduce you to Karen." David and Kareem stopped what they were doing. "This is Kareem. And," I grinned, "that's David." She shook hands with Kareem and then David. But when David and Karen shook hands, I could sense something between them. I had expected this.

David was gorgeous with his baby face, chocolate-brown eyes, and cute smile. He had a nice body, too, but he was like a big brother to me, plus, he had never given me any indication that he liked me. And Karen, that girl was a knockout with light-brown eyes, dark brown hair, and caramel-complexioned skin. She was also thin and lean. I figured they were both single, so maybe I could play matchmaker.

"We'll, I'll letchu guys get back to unpacking," I said as me and Karen started walking back out. I led her into my room and closed the door behind us.

"How did you say you knew David again?" Karen asked as she sat down on my bed. I smiled.

"His mom and my mom have been best friends since before we were born, and as a result of that, we sort of became friends, too." I went into my walk-in closet and pulled out a photo album. "See?"

"Oh, y'all were so cute." She paused as she turned the

page. "Have you and him ever . . ."

"Nope. He's all yours." I sat down next to her.

"What do you mean?" she asked, tryna play dumb.

"I saw the way y'all were lookin' at each other," I said with a smile as I nudged her in the side with my elbow.

"Yeah, he is a cutie. But have you forgotten about Tony?"

"No, but I thought you guys broke up." She smiled.

"We did, but we kind of reconciled a couple days ago."

"When were you gonna tell me this?" I asked with frown.

"I just did, and please don't look at me like that."

"Well, girl, you know that I do not like him."

"Butchu should've seen him the other night. He was so sweet."

"He's always sweet when he wants you back, 'Ren," I said with a sigh. There was a knock at my bedroom door and I got up to answer it. I smiled at David. He held his stomach.

"Hey, I been at the studio all day and I haven't eaten anything."

"Say no more," I said. I looked back at 'Ren. "I'll be right back." She nodded as she lay back on my bed.

"I said you guys could make yourselves at home," I said to David as I ran downstairs with him behind me. "You should've just raided the kitchen."

"This is my first day here," he said with a chuckle as we reached the kitchen. "Felt kinda weird." I looked in the fridge.

"What're you in the mood for? I been on this health food kick, but I'm sure we can find somethin'." I pulled out a container of rice and peas and put it on the counter. "Ah. Here we are. I'm sure there's some barbecue chicken in there too."

"That's what I'm talkin' 'bout."

I took the other container out and then walked over to the cupboard to grab two plates.

"So," David started. *Hmph*, I thought, *he's beating*

around the bush. He must be about to ask me about Karen. I looked into his eyes. He had my full attention. "Your friend Karen is pretty," he said.

"I know," I said with a smile. "I thought you'd like her." I started dishing out food.

"So what's the deal with her? You gon' hook me up?" he asked as he smiled back. I sucked my teeth.

"I wanted to, but she just made up with her jerk of a boyfriend."

"You don't like dude, huh."

"Not at all." I handed him a full plate and pointed toward the microwave. "I'll see what I can do," I told him with another smile.

"That's why you're my girl," he said with a grin as he heated up his plate. "Speakin' of hookups," he said as he looked back into my face, "Kareem is feelin' you."

"Oh, yeah? Did you let 'im know the deal?"

"What, that you're not the relationship type?" I nodded. "No, but I don't think that'll be an issue. He's not really into relationships either from what I've seen."

"Well, maybe if 'Ren comes to her senses, we can all go on a double date or somethin'." He nodded and I handed him Kareem's plate. "Hey, 'Ren!" I called. She appeared a second later. "You want somethin' to eat, girl?" She nodded and I shared her a plate.

I walked downstairs to my kitchen the next morning and David was knocking on the backdoor. I opened it for him.

"Remind me to get keys made for you today," I said as I let him in. "Where you comin' from?"

"I just went for a run," he said as looked in the fridge for a bottle of water. He took a large gulp and then looked at me. "You know it's my routine every morning. Gotta keep the body tight."

"I guess, but I've always hated running."

"So, what'd you do to get so thin?" he asked.

"Nothin' much. Stopped eating so much, and changed

some of the things I was eating a little. And you know I dance like every chance I get. My routine might be why I'm not as thin as I'd like to be."

"What?" David asked, surprised.

"I said I'm not as thin as I'd like to be."

"Please, girl, you look good."

"I look alright." He shook his head.

"No, you look damn good. With your figure, you prob'ly stop traffic." I blushed. "I'm serious. You're fine just the way you are. Don't go losin' those assets 'cuz you think you should be skinnier. Plus, you were already pretty, so now . . ." He winked at me. I smiled.

"Thanks, David. I'ma keep you around. You give me like a huge self-esteem boost."

"Just tellin' the truth," he said as he walked out of the kitchen on his way to the shower.

David

I went back downstairs after taking my shower. Kia was still in her PJs—plaid pants with a tank top. Her hair was up in a messy ponytail. She was sitting on the couch with her legs crossed, eating a bowl of Coco Puffs, and watching cartoons. I laughed at the familiar scene. This had been our Saturday morning routine since, forever.

"You haven't changed a bit," I commented as I walked over and sat next to her.

She grinned at me and gestured at the cereal box on the coffee table.

"Want some?" she asked, her mouth half full.

I shook my head and smiled back. I looked at the TV.

"What?!" I exclaimed. "*The Smurfs*? I haven't seen this in a minute. They don't show the old stuff in New York anymore, remember? We didn't have anything to watch the last time you were there."

"Oh, they don't show them here either," she told me with a smile as she got up. "But I got that covered." She went over to her entertainment center and started pulling out

DVDs. "*Fat Albert, Snorks, Flintstones,* and *Flintstone Kids.* I think I got every *Scooby* made, *He-Man,* let's see what else. Like all the Hanna-Barbera stuff, *Yogi* . . . I got everything over here."

"Ya not lyin'," I said as I picked up one of the DVDs. "Goddamn. Where'd you find these?" She grinned at me again.

"eBay." I laughed.

"You're somethin' else, girl."

"Thanks," she said as she sat back next to me. "I try."

My cell phone rang just then. It was Kareem. I picked up and talked to him briefly.

"I gotta go. Work to do at the studio."

"Aww," she said, "I thought maybe we could chill like old times." I shrugged.

"Sorry, but tell you what, I'll definitely meet you on this couch same time next week. I promise." She smiled.

"Sounds like a date. What're you doin' later?"

"Nothin'. Why?"

"'Cuz my mother is having one of her famous family dinners. Liyah's got a new boyfriend she's bringing over. My dad will even be there."

Mr. Haughton was one of the coolest old dudes I knew. That man was the ultimate playa. It was probably why he and Kia's mom were no longer together, although they remained good friends. I hadn't seen him since I was in high school.

"Oh word?" I said. "What time?"

"Like around five."

"Aight, then, I'll be there."

"Don't be late. I'll see you lata."

"Lata," I replied as I walked out the door.

CHAPTER 2

David

I walked up to the house with the blue shutters and smiled. It was good to be back. This place had been like a second home to me.

"David," Miss Anita, Kia's mother, called when I stepped onto the deck. "How are you, sweetie?" She was cooking steak on the grill. I smiled as we hugged.

"Good. How are you?"

"The same. Haven't talked to your mother in a few weeks. How is she?" I shrugged.

"Mom will always be Mom. She's doin' real good."

"I heard you graduated with a 4.0." I grinned.

"Yeah."

"That's really good. Now you have something to fall back on while you pursue your music."

"Oh, Kia told you, huh?" She nodded.

"It's good to see y'all finally workin' together."

"That isn't who I think it is, is it?" I heard a female voice say from behind me.

I turned to see Kia's sister standing in front of me as she stepped out onto the deck. We embraced.

"How are you?" she asked.

"Good," I told her when we pulled away.

"Step back so I can check you out, boy." I did. "When did you get so handsome?"

I laughed as a tall dude walked out of the house holdin' some barbecue sauce for Miss Anita. He handed it to her.

"Who's handsome?" he asked Liyah, and she smiled. He put his arm around her and looked at me.

"Don't get jealous, baby. This is just David. I told you about him." She gestured at him. "David, this is my boyfriend, Robert." I shook his hand.

"Nice to meet you, man." He just smiled and nodded. "Kia in the house?" I asked. Liyah shook her head.

"She ain't here yet." I smirked.

"Figures. She tells me not to be late, and she's the one that's not here."

"I heard that!" Kia's voice called from the side of the house. Then she walked up the steps with a smile. Her long, brown hair was curled and she wore a pair of jeans, some white flip-flops, and a white, loose-fitting blouse. She put her dark sunglasses on her head and looked up at me. "And for your info, I was on time, but"—she held up the grocery bags in her hands—"I had to stop at the store for Momma. Thank you very much."

"Whatever," I said with a shake of my head.

She pushed past me playfully as she handed the bags to her mother. I shoved her back.

"Cut it out, you two," Miss Anita said with her back turned. Kia stuck her tongue out at me and I stuck mine back.

"Oh my god," Liyah said. "I just had a flashback." We all laughed.

Kia walked up to Liyah and her boyfriend. She stuck out her hand.

"Is this Robert?" she asked with a smile.

"Yes," Liyah said. She looked up at him. "This is my little sister, Kia."

"Nice to finally meet you," Robert said as he shook her hand.

"You too," Kia said. She walked into the house then and I followed her into the kitchen. "So, how long do you think this one'll last?" she asked me with a grin. Liyah was notorious for her failing relationships. I chuckled.

"I give it six months." She giggled.

"Betchu a hundred bucks it won't last more than a

year." I smiled.

"You're on." We shook on it. I looked around. "Talk about flashbacks," I commented. "Ah, man, I haven't been in this house in forever."

"It's like a time warp, huh?" I nodded. We both walked over to her old bedroom, and she opened the door. It was pretty much the same as the last time I saw it, like it was just waiting for her to come back home. She smiled and sat down on the bed. She lay back and I went to lie next to her. I chuckled as I remembered something.

"What's so funny?" she asked.

"I just remembered the time I caught you in here with that pretty boy. What was his name?"

She hit me in the arm, but laughed too.

"His name was Brian. And it's not funny. I had to pay you fifty bucks not to say anything to Momma." I laughed harder.

"Oh, yeah. I used the money to take out Missy." She giggled.

"Ya damn con artist. Left me broke for the rest of the week."

"Hate the game, baby. Hate the game," I said with a smile.

"Oh, please," she said. I wasn't lookin' at her, but I'm positive she rolled her eyes.

That's when we heard a deep, almost booming voice coming from the kitchen. Kia looked at me with a big grin on her face.

"Daddy," she said.

She hopped up and walked out as I followed. Mr. Haughton and his ex-wife were havin' a lighthearted argument about who threw down when it came to barbecue.

"Come on now, 'Nita," Mr. Haughton said. "You and I both know can't nobody do it like me. Just hand the brush to me and lemme work it out, woman."

"Oh, please," Miss Anita said with a giggle and a roll of her eyes. *You can see where Kia gets it from,* I thought.

"Hey, baby," he said to Kia when he noticed us standing over by the hall. She practically skipped over to him. She had always been a daddy's little girl, and she seemed to revert back to that every time she saw her father. They hugged and he kissed her forehead. "How's my baby girl doin'?"

"Good," she said, still grinning. Mr. Haughton looked over at me then.

"This grown man can't be little David," he said as he looked me over in shock.

I chuckled and walked over to shake his hand.

"How you doin', sir?" I asked.

"Not bad, son, not bad at all."

"Dinner will be ready soon," Kia's mother interjected.

"Oh, I can't wait," I said. "I missed your cooking, Miss Anita." She smiled at me.

"Ten minutes," she said as she walked out to the back porch.

"How 'bout a game of poker?" Kia suggested with a grin after we'd all eaten.

There was a chorus of "oh no's," "uh-uh's," and "hell no's." She grabbed the pack of cards from the coffee table and giggled as she opened the box.

"Come on, y'all, we can play with partners."

"That's exactly the reason no one wants to play," Liyah said. "You and David always cheat."

Kia glanced at me and I smiled at her. Now, we'd never really cheated, per se. It's just that we knew each other so well that we were just in sync like that. We could read each other's every expression.

"Damn, it's like that?" Robert asked.

"No," Kia answered. "Don't let her scare you."

"We've never cheated," I said.

"Yeah, right," Miss Anita said. "I really don't feel like goin' broke tonight."

"OK then," Kia said. "How 'bout Monopoly?" She pulled out that game and everyone agreed.

"But you and Dave sit across from each other," Liyah said.

"Why?" I asked.

"So you won't be able to slip money to each other."

Kia and I laughed. Monopoly was the only game we did cheat at, I swear. We both nodded our heads and promised to be good.

That didn't stop Kia from kickin' all our asses though.

"Boardwalk!" she shouted as soon as her dad's thimble landed on her property.

"Oh no," Mr. Haughton groaned.

"None of that grumbling!" Kia shouted. "Just gimme my money!" He reluctantly handed her his last play hundred-dollar bill. "Thank you," she said as she snatched it out of his hands. Liyah giggled and stood up with Robert.

"On that note, I think it's time for us to go," she said. She hugged and kissed everyone. "It's been real, people," she said, and then she and her man walked out.

"I guess that's our cue, too," Kia said as we stood. We said our goodbyes and I followed her home in my car.

"Ay," I said when we stepped into the living room. "I have my first video shoot tomorrow. Wanna roll wit' me?" She smiled.

"OK, cool. What time?"

"We start shooting in the afternoon." She nodded.

"Aight then." She yawned. "I'm so sleepy. I'll see you in the morning."

I nodded and followed her upstairs.

I opened the front door for Kareem the next morning.

"What's good, man?" I said as we gave each other dap

"Chillin'," he replied as he walked inside. "I just came from the set, tryna get everything squared away."

"Oh word?" I said as I walked over to the TV. I turned on my Xbox, which I had brought with me to Cali, and held up the second controller for him. He nodded and I handed it over. "Is everything straight over there?"

"Yeah." He sat down on the couch and I sat next to him. "They were running a little late, but I guess they fixed whatever it was. Things should be ready by the time we get there."

I nodded and started the game.

Kia walked down the steps just then. Her hair was up in a ponytail and she wore no makeup. She had on tight, gray biker shorts and black T-shirt that was tied at the waist. Her stomach was flat, but she didn't have body-builder abs or anything like that. And she'd pierced her belly button. Her tiny waist curved down to her sexy hips, and her ass . . . my god. I'd never seen her like that.

She smiled at us, that pretty smile.

"Morning, y'all," she said as she walked into the kitchen.

"Morning," Kareem and I said in unison. Our mouths were wide open and our heads crooked to the side to see into the kitchen. Kareem tapped me on my arm.

"I thought you said you didn't see her like that, man," he said quietly when I looked at him. I smiled.

"I didn't, but goddamn," I said. "This is a new thing for me. She didn't look like that when we were younger." He laughed as we resumed our game.

"So if you could turn back time and she looked the way she does now? Would you hit that?"

"Do I even have to answer that question?"

We both laughed and bumped fists.

"So did you put in a good word for me or what?" Kareem asked.

"Yeah, I talked to her about it. She was up for it. You just need to go ask her out, dawg."

"Just like that? I shouldn't have an approach or anything?" I shook my head.

"She's a pretty straight forward type of girl."

"Really? Like how straight forward?"

"There's no need to beat around the bush with her in any aspect."

"Really?" he said again. He smiled at the thought and I kinda wished I hadn't said anything.

"But don't take advantage of her, man," I said crossly.

"I won't," he said, looking at me innocently like he

wasn't just thinking about getting her into bed not one minute ago.

"I'm serious," I told him.

"Yo, Dave, you should know I'm not like that, aight? I'll only go as far as she wants to go. There's no need to worry."

I nodded and left it at that as we continued our game.

Kia

Kareem walked up to me after the video shoot later on that day.

"Wassup?" I said. He smiled.

"I was just wondering what you were doing after this."

I looked into his eyes. They were green, and he was cute—light-skinned with brown, wavy hair. Body wasn't bad either. I started thinkin' of the possibilities. It happened that quickly. I smiled back coyly.

"Nothin'. Why? Whatchu got in mind?"

"Oh, I'm thinkin' of many things," he flirted back. "But it's on you." I licked my lips.

"You're stayin' in a hotel, right?" He nodded. "I have to change outta these clothes, but I definitely wanna hook up. Can I meet you there?"

"I'll do you one better," he said. He reached into the pocket of his jeans and pulled out a card. He handed it to me and I smiled. David musta told him that I ain't wit' the bullshit, 'cuz he is mighty bold. "Come see me as soon as you're done, OK?" I nodded and he leaned toward me. I held his chin and kissed him softly. His lips were juicy and his breath smelled like peppermint.

"See you lata." He grinned.

"Bye."

I noticed David watching us from my left and looked at him. He raised his eyebrows at me. Kareem looked at him too and we both smiled. Kareem walked away then and I looked at David. He just shook his head with a slight smile.

Guess I was doing what was expected of me. I grinned and walked into my dressing room.

Less than an hour later I unlocked the door to Kareem's suite. It was a beautiful room. He had all the perks—a huge flat screen TV and a balcony with a view of LA. I noticed that you could even see the Hollywood sign as I walked closer to the open doors. He had D'Angelo playing "How Does it Feel," and I smiled as I walked into the bedroom. He was lying on the bed, the lights were dim, and he grinned as I stepped inside.

I didn't say anything as I slipped off my sneakers. I then took off my shirt and slowly slid off my jeans. And there I stood in an off-white, front-hook bra and thong set, which perfectly stood out against my dark skin. His smile grew wider as he patted the spot next to him. I smiled back and crawled up the bed beside him where I lay on my back.

He stroked my waistline and then pulled off his shirt and jeans. He unhooked my bra and sucked on each nipple slowly. After pulling off my thong, he got on top of me. We kissed each other, and he was an extremely good kisser. By the time his lips left mine, I was ready. I helped him get off his boxers, then I grabbed a condom from the nightstand, opened it, and rolled it on. He had a lot to work with. He looked shocked but enticed by my boldness. I just smiled and waited to feel him move inside me. But when he did, I didn't feel much of anything, and I knew there was something wrong.

"Is it in yet?" I asked quietly. He sighed.

"Yeah, but I, uh, kind of lost my hard-on." I sighed too as he moved off me. "I don't know what happened."

I started thinkin' of logical reasons.

"Did I scare you when I—"

"No," he said, looking into my eyes. He smiled. "I liked that." I smiled back.

"Are you nervous or something?"

"Yeah, a little bit, but I've been nervous before and *never* had this problem."

"Maybe we just"—I shrugged—"moved too fast." I

kissed his lips. "Maybe we should work on foreplay a little bit." He smiled again and kissed me. I moaned softly when he moved to my neck and stroked my pussy. He slid a finger inside me and I moaned a little louder. I held his head as he sucked one of my nipples. "Ooh, that feels so good, Kareem," I said. I kissed him again and started to play with his balls. It was his turn to moan. I moved to stroke his dick and it definitely felt like someone was ready. I guess he thought so too because he aggressively got on top of me. He put my leg over his shoulder and moved inside me. I gasped. He was so deep, but then he thrust a couple times, and once again, I couldn't feel anything.

He pulled out and lay beside me again, frustrated. I started to get insecure.

"Is it me?" I asked. He propped himself on his elbow.

"No, it's definitely not you." I propped myself up too.

"But you're fine when you're not inside me," I insisted.

"Kia, trust me, you are one of the most sexy women that I've been with. And I want you so badly."

"I want you, too." I kissed his lips. "What can I do to make this last for the both of us?" I smiled as I pushed him back gently and got on top of him. He licked his lips.

"This is a great start." I kissed him deeply. Then I grinded my hips against his dick as I licked one of his nipples. I felt him grow hard again and wasted no time putting it inside me. I bounced up and down as he moaned and grabbed for my breasts. It actually felt like it might last this time. I moved to kiss his neck and then moved up to his ear.

"Ooh, not the ear," he moaned. Then I felt his muscles tense. I froze and spoke into his ear.

"Kareem, did you just . . ."

He hesitated before answering me.

"Yes," he finally admitted.

"Oh, you've got to be kidding me," I said as I got up off him. I had been more than patient with him, but now, I was pissed and very sexually frustrated. I wasn't tryna hide it either.

"Kia, wait." He grabbed my hand and I pulled away. I walked over to my pile of clothing and started to get dressed.

"I can't believe this," I mumbled to myself.

"Kia, don't go. I'm sorry," he said helplessly. All the confidence that had been in him earlier was gone.

I put my hand up as he started to stand.

"Don't get up." I threw the key card on the bed. "I'll see myself out."

David was asleep on the couch when I walked into my condo. He awoke to the sound of my keys being dropped on the table.

"Hey," he said. He looked at the clock on the DVD player. Only one o'clock. "Aren'tchu home a little early?" he asked.

I just nodded as I put my sneakers in the front closet.

"Bad night?" he asked. I thought about an answer as I sat down next to him.

"Not bad," I said. "More like disappointing."

"What happened?"

I smirked.

"Nothing. Nothing at all," I told him.

"Really?" David asked in surprise. "Y'all seemed hot and heavy earlier."

"Yeah, well, appearances can be deceiving." He raised his eyebrows at me and I just shook my head as I got up. "Long story. I'm 'bout to head to bed. I'm beat. I'll see you in the morning." David nodded and I walked toward the stairs.

There was a knock at the front door the next morning and I went to answer it. Kareem stood there. I stepped back with a slight smile and held my hand out for him to come in. I walked into the kitchen and he followed. I grabbed an apple and bit into it as I sat on the counter. He looked into my eyes.

"Still mad at me?" he asked. I took another bite of my apple and shook my head.

"I'm sorry," he said.

"Don't worry about it," I told him as I waved it off.

"I don't know what happened. For some reason, nothing went right."

"Kareem, it's really OK."

"Maybe if I had a second chance, we could—" I shook my head. "Why not?"

"'Cuz I don't do second chances," I explained. He was confused.

"Why?"

"I just don't. Nothing against you or anything."

"Kia—" he started, but never finished because we heard David's footsteps coming down the stairs. He walked into the kitchen.

"Wassup, man?" David said. He and Kareem bumped fists as I hopped down from the counter. David looked at both of us, reading our expressions. "Is it gonna be weird between y'all two now?"

"No," I answered for the both of us. I looked at Kareem and smiled. "Because nothing happened, right?" Kareem nodded.

"Yeah, we're cool," he said, even though I could see that he was aggravated, mad because the possibility of redeeming himself was shot down.

I felt a little bad, but those were the breaks. What could I say? After what happened, I just didn't feel as attracted to him as I did before. It happened that quickly.

"I'll see y'all later," I said and took another bite of my apple as I walked up to my room.

CHAPTER 3

Kia

Crash!

I sat upright in my bed, scared out of my deep sleep a few weeks later.

What the fuck was that? I wondered. I could definitely hear movement in my kitchen at three AM. I looked around my room for a weapon, but couldn't think of anything I could use. It wasn't like I had a bat stashed somewhere. Then I thought of going to wake David.

I got up and walked toward my door quietly. I opened it slowly and looked out in the hall, only to see that David was already awake. He grabbed my hand as we both crept down the hall and down the stairs. We could see a figure in the darkness when we got to the kitchen. It was crouched over by the sink. David flipped on the light.

Karen stood upright and I placed my hand over my chest in relief.

"Jesus Christ, 'Ren," I said. "You scared the shit outta us."

"Sorry," she said, crouching to pick up what she had dropped. "I didn't wanna wake you guys, so I used my key to get in. And then I stubbed my toe and dropped the pot I was carryin'."

David frowned, very much agitated to have been woken up in the middle of the night. He shook his head and looked down at me with sleepy eyes.

"Good night, y'all," he said. He started back up the stairs.

"Sorry," 'Ren called again as she stood up.

"Mmph," he grunted as he walked down the hall. I smiled and that's when I noticed Karen's eyes.

"You been cryin'?" I asked in concern. She looked at me sadly as she stooped back down. "What happened?" I went to help her clean up the mess she made.

"Nothin'," she responded. She tried to look away, but I held her chin and turned her face toward mine.

"Seriously," I said. She didn't answer as we both stood. "This wouldn't have anything to do with Tony, would it?"

A tear fell from her eye just at the mention of his name.

"Come on," I said as I put my arm around her and led her to the living room. We sat on the couch. "Tell me what happened."

"Basically I found out that he's still sleeping with his baby's mama." I shook my head.

"I told you that man wasn't no good." She put her head in her hands.

"But you don't understand, Kia. He is good when we're together. Things are all good."

"Yeah, until he steps out on you again. Why do you let him do this to you?" She sat upright again and shrugged.

"Because I love him. And despite what you or anyone else thinks, I know he loves me too."

"He loves you so much that he's sleeping with some-one else," I said flatly.

"You just don't understand—"

"You're damn right I don't understand," I inter-rupted. "You deserve so much better than this jerk that couldn't care less about what he's doing to you."

"It's complicated."

"Obviously." I shook my head. "He's playin' you for a fool and he'll keep doin' it until you put your foot down. You know this shit ain't right." She didn't respond and I looked away from her, shaking my head again. I rubbed my temples. She was giving me a headache. I didn't have the patience to try to speak anymore sense into her; I was way too tired. "Listen," I said as I stood up, "I'll just see you in the morning." I looked at the clock. "Or rather, in a few hours."

She nodded.

Karen and I didn't say much of anything to each other that morning.

We were quietly sitting on the couch, watching TV when David walked through the backdoor. He grabbed a bottle of water from the refrigerator and walked into the living room.

"Good morning," he said with a grin. We both smiled at him. He was all sweaty as he gulped down his water. His athletic body was tight in the wife-beater and basketball shorts he wore. He'd taken out his braids and his hair was pulled back by an elastic.

"Morning," I said back.

"You think you can braid my hair after I come out the shower?" he asked me.

"Umm, I have a dance class to teach in a little while. You would have to wash and blow dry it quick." He nodded.

"OK, that won't take me long." He ran upstairs, givin' us full view of his tight butt with each stride.

"That man is gorgeous," 'Ren stated. I smiled.

"I know, right? He's a sweetheart, too."

"So tell me something," she started and I looked at her. "Why is it that you guys aren't together?" I shrugged as I thought about it.

"He doesn't like me like that."

"How do you know? Has he said anything?" I shook my head.

"No, I can just tell."

"What's not to like about you?"

"I don't know. He's never dropped any hints or anything."

"You keep putting the focus on him. You like him or something?"

"I never said that." She smiled.

"You never denied it either. You sayin' you would turn that beautiful man down even if he did like you?" I grinned.

"I didn't say all that. That would just be stupid."

"That's what I thought."

"David and I have been close forever, but it will never be anymore than what it is. He still sees me as that little girl he knew way back when."

"Yeah, but y'all are all grown up now. Believe me, it's only a matter of time before he sees the woman that you've grown up to be, if he hasn't already noticed. You'll see."

I never got a chance to contest Karen's statements because David was coming back down the stairs. His 'fro was all blown out.

"Damn, that was quick," I said.

He handed me a comb and some grease. Then he sat down between my legs.

"Told you it wouldn't take me long," he said.

I just smiled as I started to part his hair and tried to ignore the looks that Karen was giving us.

After I was done braiding, Karen and I changed into loose clothing and got ready to go to the dance studio.

"Yo 'Ren!" I called upstairs from the living room. "I'll be in the car, OK?"

"Aight!" she yelled back. "Be down there in like two seconds!" I picked up my dance bag by the closet door.

"See you later," I said to David.

"Yeah," he replied. "You still meetin' me and Kareem at the mall later, right?"

I nodded and opened the door to walk out. When I saw who stood before me, I just knew we would be late.

"Geez," I said as I sucked my teeth.

"Nice to see you too, Kia," Tony said as he invited himself inside.

David looked over at the door curiously from his spot on the couch. Tony glanced at him. I gestured at Tony and reluctantly introduced them.

"This is Karen's boyfriend, Antoine. That's my boy David." They nodded at each other.

"Karen here?" Tony asked.

"She's upstairs," I told him flatly.

"Yo, Kia, why you always so cold to me?"

"Because I don't appreciate the way you have 'Ren comin' to my place at three in the morning with tears in her eyes."

"You don't know shit about what we have," he said angrily.

"I know enough," I retorted with much attitude.

Karen came down the steps with her bag. She put it down when she noticed Tony.

"What're you doing here?" she asked as she crossed her arms. His entire expression softened.

"Can I talk to you?" he asked.

She looked at me before she answered. I glared at her, not hiding my disapproval, but she obliged anyway.

"OK," she said. She grabbed his hand. "We can talk in my room." She led him down the hall and shut the door behind them.

I dropped my bag with a shake of my head and sat down next to David.

"I might as well get comfortable."

"What is the deal with them two?" he asked.

"Tony is a straight up dog," I told him. David raised his eyebrows.

"Miss P.I.M.P. herself is judging someone else for being with more than one person?" I looked up into his eyes.

"I resent that. Him and I are in no way alike."

"Really?" he said turning to face me fully. "Why's that?"

"'Cuz I'm honest with every guy I'm with. They know what it's all about and for the most part, they don't care. I don't go sneaking behind anyone's back and I'm not hurting anyone."

"OK, but he even said it. You don't know what the situation is between them."

"I know he's sleeping with his baby's mother with no regard for how Karen feels."

"Maybe it's a comfort thing between him and his ex-girl. Maybe he's in love with Karen, but doesn't know how to break it off with the other person. Maybe he's in love with both women. Who knows?"

"So you're saying what he's doin' is right?"

"Oh no, I didn't say that at all," David replied as he sat back again. "It's still fucked up, and he shouldn't be stringin' both of them along. I just meant that sometimes things are more complicated than they seem. And you of all people should not be judging." I nodded.

"You have a point. I just don't like being the one to pick up the pieces after he's hurt her. And he just keeps doing it."

David

I was in good spirits when Kareem and I met up with Kia later that day at the mall.

"Wassup?" she said with a smile as we walked in front of Chili's. "Why you all giddy?"

"I just got a call from my label," I told her with a grin. "Apparently my album is number three on Billboard."

"That is great!" she exclaimed as she hugged me. I hugged her back.

"It all seems so unreal."

"I can only imagine," she said as we walked into the restaurant.

"You won't have to imagine. Soon you'll be up there, too."

"I can't wait," she said.

We were seated and Kareem got right down to business.

"So, me and the label are thinking with the success of the first single, and with the album doing so well, we should ride this wave. We think we should use the song we did with you as the next single," he said to Kia.

"Oh wow," she said, flattered. "I'm honored." Kareem smiled.

"I was hoping you would say that. That's why I wanted us to meet up. I was hoping that we could start workin' out the details."

"Sounds good."

We took a few minutes to look at the menu. Then we ordered our food and started to compare schedules.

Kia's phone rang when the waitress placed our food on the table. She flipped it open and clicked talk.

"Hello?" She smiled as the person on the other end responded, the kinda smile that letchu know that she was talkin' to some guy. "Hey, what's up? . . . Nothin'. I'm eatin' lunch with David. . . . Yeah . . ." She looked up and noticed us staring at her. "Excuse me, y'all," she said and walked out into the mall to speak without us being nosey. Kareem looked at me when she left.

"Yo, Kia be speakin' to a lot of dudes," he commented.

"I know, but she's always been like this. She's worse than some guys. Shit, she's worse than me," I said with a smile.

"Yeah, but she's been with like three guys in the past month or so, and that's just when I've been around." I furrowed my brow.

"So? What's your point?"

"Nothin'. Just sayin' seems like a lotta guys be runnin' up and through her." I glared at him.

"What the hell is that supposed to mean?" He shrugged.

"It was just a comment, dawg."

"No the fuck it wasn't," I said crossly.

"Relax, it's not anything for you to get all mad about."

"I'm not s'posed to get mad when you're sitting here talking about her like she's some kinda hoe? She's like family to me, dawg, and it ain't right for you to make comments about shit you don't know about. What, you mad 'cuz shit didn't work out between y'all?"

"No," he said sharply, frowning at me. He sighed. "Look, I'm sorry if you took what I said to heart. I knew you were protective of her, but not to this degree. I honestly didn't mean anything by what I said."

"That ain't right, man. If she was a dude, this wouldn't even be an issue."

"OK, damn. I said I was sorry."

I nodded just as Kia came back and sat down next to me.

"Ooh," she said as she grabbed her fork. "I am so hungry." She glanced at both of us, sensing the thick tension that had risen while she was gone. "What's wrong with you two?"

"Nothin'," I answered for both of us.

She looked across the table at Kareem and then back into my eyes.

"You sure?"

"Everything's straight. Don't worry about it," Kareem said.

I went to the gym and shot some hoops to clear my head after we left the mall. As wrong as Kareem was to speak that way about Kia, he'd given me a lot to think about. It made me worry more than anything, especially because she showed absolutely no signs of slowing down.

It was around eight-thirty when I drove home. I dropped my keys on the table and took off my sneakers. I walked up to Kia's bedroom door. The lights were on and it was halfway open. I knocked because I didn't see her.

"David? That you?" she called from her bathroom and I walked in.

"Yeah, it's me."

"Good," she said as she walked over to me. Her hair was curled and pinned up. She was barefoot and had on this white, satin dress that beautifully contrasted with her skin color. She held it to her breasts and turned her back toward me to reveal an unclosed zipper. "Zip me up, please?" I fas-

ANJEL

tened her dress.

"Where you goin' tonight?" I asked. She turned to face me with a smile.

"I met this gorgeous guy at the club the other night. He's taking me out." She walked over to her dresser and picked up a simple silver necklace. I walked over without a word and clipped it on for her. "Damn," she said as she noticed my expression in the mirror. "Why you look so serious?"

I smiled slightly as I sat down on her bed.

"Can I ask you a personal question?" She giggled a little as she turned to look at me.

"I think we know each other a little too well to be offended by 'personal' questions, David. Go ahead and ask."

"OK," I said and then just got straight to it. "Do you sleep with all these guys thatchu go out with?"

"Not all of them," she responded with a smile. "But I'm not innocent either. I *do* have sex."

"Do you use protection every time?" I asked.

"Yes, of course. You've seen me take the pill."

"I'm not talkin' about the pill, Chunky. Do you use condoms, dental dams, spermicidal lubricant?"

She looked at me sincerely then. I guess she sensed my concern.

"Trust me, I protect myself every single time I have sex, OK? Why are you asking me this anyway?" I smiled and thought about the many times we'd been in this same situation—Kia goin' out and me playin' the concerned older brother.

"Can't a big brother be worried?" I asked.

"Of course, but there is no need to be. I can handle myself." There was knock on the front door. "Oh shoot, that's Terrance and I'm not even ready. Go down and stall for me." I nodded as I headed out the door. "By the way," she called and I faced her in the doorway. "This guy does actually think that you're my brother, so please be nice." I smirked.

"Oh, trust, I'll be as nice as can be."

I ran downstairs and opened up the front door. I

looked Terrance over skeptically. Couldn't have been more than five-ten. His brown skin was a little darker than mine and he was skinny, at least compared to me. I decided to entertain myself while we waited for Kia to come downstairs. He smiled as I let him in. He held out his hand.

"David, right?" he said. "I've heard a lot aboutchu." I gave him dap.

"Really? Kia hasn't mentioned anything about you," I said without returning his smile. He looked surprised by my offbeat comment.

"Well, we just met so . . ." He shrugged.

I nodded and rubbed my chin as I asked my next question.

"Where you taking her tonight?"

"To a play. She said she was into dance and everything, so I figured she'd like it."

"Nice move. You working hard to get into them panties, huh." He looked taken aback.

"What?" I smiled slightly.

"I'm sayin', a play? That is strictly a playa's move, don'tchu think? I should be takin' notes."

"I guess so . . ." My smile faded.

"So you *are* tryna get some ass tonight?"

"No, I mean, uh . . ."

"You mean what? You're planning on taking advantage of my sister?"

"Naw, man. It ain't even like that." I looked at him fiercely as I cracked my knuckles.

"Betta not be. 'Cuz if I hear one word aboutchu treating her any less than the lady that she is tonight, you gonna have to deal wit' me. Got it?"

He nodded just as Kia came down the steps.

"Hey," she said as she walked over to us. She smiled at Terrance and gave him a kiss on the cheek. He glanced at me as she did this. She noticed his expression as he pulled away and looked up at me. She punched me in the arm. "I told you to be nice. What'd you say to him?"

I chuckled as I rubbed my bicep.

"Nothin', I swear. I was just havin' a little fun with him."

"I bet." She looked back at Terrance. "Don't pay him any attention, OK? Trust me, he's not as tough as he looks."

"Oh, trust *me*, Terrance," I said, still playing my big brother role, "listening to *her* is liable to getchu hurt."

"OK, *enough*, David." I laughed to myself as she gestured at the door. Terrance walked out and she looked back at me. She giggled a little. "I can't believe you." I shrugged as I smiled back. "Don't wait up. Good night."

I nodded and then shut the door behind her.

I sat down on the couch and the phone rang as soon as I turned on the TV. I picked it up, looked at the ID, and smiled.

"Hello?"

"How's my favorite son doing?" I heard my mother's voice ask.

I laughed. It was good to hear her voice. She was an RN that worked nights, so we were kinda on opposite schedules. It was hard to catch each other.

"Good, Mom. How've you been?"

"Great. I miss you, though."

"I miss you, too."

"How are things out there?"

"Really good. I'm working a lot. The schedule seems to get more hectic by the day. But now that my single is number three on the charts, I guess I have to get used to that, 'cuz it'll only get worse."

"Number three, huh? Who's above you?" I smiled.

"Usher and some rock group," I said with a chuckle.

"Well, I'm proud of you, sweetie."

"Thanks, Mom."

"So, how's Kia?"

"The same as always. That girl will never change. As a matter of fact, she's out on a date as we speak." Mom laughed.

"You're right. She'll always be the same. But you and her are getting along and everything?"

"Of course. We always have."

"Well, you know I have to check and make sure."

"Yeah. Actually, I never told you, huh? Kia's lost madd weight."

"Really? How's she look?"

"I can't lie. She looks damn good." My mother chuckled at my response.

"Really now," she said again. "So?"

I smiled. "So what?"

"What does this mean for you guys?"

"Nothing," I told her. "I mean, she's still goin' through this player thing."

"Butchu have thought about it?"

I could almost hear her grinning through the phone. I shook my head, but told the truth.

"Yeah, I have."

"Well, I think you should make your move. She's always been beautiful. I bet she's a knockout now."

I shook my head again with another smile on my face. My mother was a trip. My cell phone rang before I could respond, though.

"Hold on a sec, Mom," I said. "My cell is ringing." I opened it and clicked on. "Hello?"

"Wassup, playa?" Kareem said on the other end. "Whatchu doin' tonight?" he asked casually, and all the bullshit from earlier was squashed that easy. We never did dwell on things for very long.

"Nothin', man," I replied. "Why? What's poppin' tonight, dawg?"

"Well, s'posed to be a hott party goin' down at Soho later. Bar's free 'til ten and everything."

"Oh word?"

"Yeah. So I figure, we should go, 'cuz once you blow up we won't be able to really party on this level, ya know? It'll be all VIP and shit. And you know they don't party like the people do." I laughed.

"Yeah. Aight, then. I'm on the phone wit' my mom right now, but come through. I should be ready by the time you get here."

"OK, cool. Lata."

"Lata." I hung up and put the other phone back to my ear. "Hello?"

"I'm still here," my mother said.

"Yeah, that was Kareem."

"I figured. You seem to speak another language when you guys talk." I laughed again.

"I guess. He wants to go out, so I'm gonna have to call you later."

"Alright then. Make sure you do. I love you, sweetie."

"I love you, too. Bye."

"Bye-bye."

It was live at the club. And the girls . . . ah, man. I didn't realize how horny I actually was until I stepped into the place and danced with a few women. I hadn't had sex since I came to Cali, and that was about a month or two ago. Needless to say, that became my mission: find someone to bring home. I wasn't proud of myself, but hey, when you needed it, you needed it.

I actually met someone while I was getting a drink at the bar. She was standing next to me asking for a Sex on the Beach. Coincidence? I thought not. I glanced over at her and checked her out while the bartenders filled our glasses. Her skin was the color of peanut butter. She had on this pink dress with the back out. It hugged her ass just right. Her chest wasn't as big as I usually liked 'em, but it would do.

She noticed me gazing at her and smiled up at me after taking a sip of her drink. Lips were juicy. I smiled back.

"You just gon' stare at me and not say nothin'?" she asked, and there was no mistakin' the east coast I heard in her voice. I held out my hand.

"Wassup? I'm David," I said. "You are?"

"Chante," she said as she shook my hand with a coy smile.

"Where you from, Chante?" I asked.

"Connecticut."

"Ah, I knew it. I'm from Brooklyn. What brings you way out here?"

"Visiting family. You?"

"I'm actually pursuin' a music career right now." She grinned.

"Isn't everyone pursuin' somethin' in LA?" I laughed.

"Yeah."

We continued to make small talk until we finished our drinks. Then we went out onto the floor and danced until she whispered in my ear that she was ready to leave. I let her know that I hadn't driven up there, but she was cool with it. I let Kareem know I was leavin' and we were on our way.

When we got to Kia's spot, she parked next to my car in the parking lot. I noticed that Kia wasn't home yet by the darkness inside the condo. I opened the front door and turned on the lamp. Chante looked around as she stepped inside.

"Nice place," she commented. I nodded.

"Yeah, I'm stayin' with a friend," I told her. She nodded back and then pulled me into her.

"You know I been wantin' to kiss you all night, right?" I smiled.

"Word?" I asked in a low tone as our lips touched. She nodded again and grinned. I kissed her softly and then grabbed her hand. "Come on." I led the way up the stairs.

She kissed me eagerly when we got to my room. She unbuttoned my shirt and slid it off. I pushed up her dress and squeezed her ass. She unbuckled my belt and pulled on my jeans. I grabbed a condom out of my pocket before my jeans dropped to floor. She turned me around and pushed me on the bed. I smiled up at her in the darkness. She slipped outta her dress and I stood at attention. I opened the condom wrapper with my teeth and rolled it on. She was stark naked as she climbed on top of me.

I moaned loudly as she sat down on my dick. I couldn't help it, that shit felt good as she rode me. I sat up and licked her nipples. I sucked each one into to my mouth as I grabbed her waist and held her as she bounced.

Then I took control and laid her on her back. I kissed her neck and thrust 'til she screamed in pleasure. Her nails dug into my back each time she came, and then finally, I let go, too.

I rolled off her, spent. We both passed out after a few moments.

Kia

I looked at the stage in awe that night. I was trying not to show how much I really liked watching the ballet, but I don't think I did a very good job. I don't know how Terrance really felt about watching the play, but I definitely appreciated the gesture.

He held my hand and led the way out when it was over.

"Thank you for bringing me here," I said when we got outside. He smiled as we walked over to his Lex.

"No problem," he said. "I'm glad you liked it." I nodded.

"I did, but it musta been like torture for you, huh?" He shook his head.

"It wasn't that bad." His dark brown eyes looked into mine. "Wasn't really watching the play much anyway." I looked away and blushed.

"We're really gonna have to do somethin' you like next time, though. Like go to a Lakers' game or somethin'."

"Oh, so you're already plannin' on there bein' a next time, huh?" he asked with a grin. I smiled back.

"Well, yeah. I mean, if that's alright witchu."

He nodded as he opened the passenger door for me. He walked around to the driver's side and got in.

"OK, next time we'll go to a game," he said as he started the car and drove off. "So you like basketball then?"

"Oh yeah," I said. "Me and David used to go see the Lakers play the Knicks when he was in town."

"You and him are real close?" I nodded.

"Can I ask you somethin'?" He looked at me as he

stopped for traffic.

"Sure, go ahead." I smiled.

"What exactly did David say to you before I came downstairs?" He chuckled as he drove.

"Nothin' major. Just doin' what a big brother should. You know, intimidation, threats of murder, the usual." He chuckled again and I laughed too.

"I'm sorry about that. Sometimes he gets a little carried away with that stuff." He laughed again.

"Don't worry about it. I have little sisters, too, so I understand how it is." I smiled.

"How many sisters do you have?" I asked.

"Two. One is about graduate from college, the other is sixteen."

"No brothers?"

"Nope. You?"

"My big sister, Liyah. I actually have a confession to make."

"What's that?" Terrance asked curiously.

"David isn't really my brother."

"Oh?"

"Yeah. I mean, he might as well be. We grew up together and he is like family to me. But I didn't wanna tell you at first 'cuz dudes be actin' funny when they find out I live with a guy."

"Ohhh, I see. Not a problem."

I looked at the clock on the dash and noticed it was still early as we headed for my place. I didn't really want the night to end yet.

"Think we could go back to your place?" I asked. He glanced at me with a smile. "I'm not ready for our date to end." He nodded.

"OK."

He drove past the entrance to my complex and headed toward his apartment.

We talked until the wee hours of the morning. And surprisingly for me, that was all. He'd been a total gentleman the entire night. He kissed me tenderly when he dropped me off, and waited for me to get fully inside before he left. I turned off the lamp on the table before I went up to my room.

David's door was shut all the way. I was a little sad. I wanted to tell him everything, but I guess it could wait until tomorrow.

I got up early the next morning and brushed my teeth. I had a busy day ahead of me. I walked out into the hall and looked down at David's door. Still shut. *Hmm, that's strange*, I thought. He was usually religious as hell about his morning runs. I didn't think too much more on it though as I walked downstairs to the kitchen.

I opened up one of the cabinets and grabbed the box of Coco Puffs. I opened the fridge and grabbed the milk, then reached for a bowl. I fixed my bowl of cereal and hoisted myself up onto the counter. I had just put a spoonful in my mouth when I heard footsteps on the stairs. But they were way too delicate to be David's. I chewed as I looked up at the entryway curiously. I almost choked on my food when a girl walked into my kitchen with one of David's T-shirts on and nothing else. She was flat-chested. She had one of those fifty-cent, I'm-going-to-the-club-thrown-in kinda weaves, and last night's makeup on. I was surprised that her nails and toes were even done.

She folded her arms across her chest, I guess in embarrassment from her lack of clothing, and looked at me strangely.

"Who are you?" she asked.

I smirked a bit and put down my bowl. I hopped off the counter.

"*I* live here," I said as I pointed to my chest. "Who are you?"

"What?" she said in surprise without answering my question. "David said he was staying with a friend." I giggled.

"And he just neglected to tell you that I was a girl." She didn't look the least bit amused.

"But you're like his sister or cousin or somethin',

right?" I shook my head.

"Nope."

"Friends with benefits?" she asked bluntly.

No this bitch didn't just ask me that. I looked at her crossly.

"That's a little personal, don'tchu think?" She rolled her eyes.

"Take that as a yes."

Who the fuck did she think she was, comin' in *my* house interrogating *me*? I didn't like her attitude. I put my finger up, ready to cuss her out.

"Listen here—" I started, but was interrupted by the backdoor opening.

David walked in and looked at both of us.

"I see you two have met," he said.

"Informally," I said, still looking at her from across the room. Miss thang narrowed her eyes at David.

"Why didn't you tell me you were staying with some woman?" She asked.

"I said I was staying with a friend, didn't I?" he said with a shrug. "What's the problem?"

"I don't know what's goin' on between y'all two," she remarked haughtily.

"Wow," I said with a shake of my head. I looked up at David. "Can I talk to you for a sec?"

He nodded and followed me to the den as she stared me down.

"OK," I began, "I'm gonna cutchu a little slack because we've never really had a huge issue in this area, but we definitely need go over some ground rules for when you bring someone home." He smiled.

"Aight."

"First of all, let 'em know the deal before they walk through the door so that I don't have any problems. These bitches need to respect me in my house. They also need to know to put on some damn clothes. I don't want these chicks flippin' on *me* 'cuz you didn't tell them shit." He chuckled.

"OK. You're right, Chunky. My badd."

I crossed my arms and smiled back.

"You should get ass more often," I told him. He grinned.

"Why's that?" I shrugged.

"I don't know. You have this whole laid-back feel aboutchu. I must say that I like it." I smiled again. "Plus, you've barely stopped grinning since you walked through the door."

He chuckled and I walked out. I went up to my room. I opened one of my drawers and pulled out an old pair of jeans with one of my tees. I walked back downstairs. David was using his charm on the girl, hugging her and kissin' her neck. She even giggled. He looked up when I walked into the kitchen. She looked back. I handed her the clothes.

"By the way, my name is Kia," I informed her. She smiled.

"Thank you. I'm Chante. Sorry about the attitude I was giving you. You know David didn't tell me anything."

"Quite alright." She went upstairs to change. I walked over to my now very soggy cereal, poured it into the sink, and ran the garbage disposal.

David looked at his watch when I turned back around.

"Aren'tchu up a little early anyway?" he asked.

"Yeah," I said as I poured a new bowl of cereal. "I'ma be working most of the day, then I'll be at Momma's house." I leaned on the counter as I started eating again.

"So, how was your date last night?" I turned and faced him with a smile.

"It was nice." He looked at me curiously.

"Wow," he said, "I don't think I've ever seen that look in your eye." I grinned.

"What look?"

"You seem like you actually like this dude." I shrugged.

"Well, I don't know, I had a good time. We even planned to go out again and he was a perfect gentleman."

"Wow," he said again as I giggled. "You look that

way and you didn't even get laid? I guess I was right last night. I *should* be takin' notes from this dude."

I laughed again as Chante came back into the room with her belongings in her hand.

"I have to go," she announced. She handed David a piece of paper. "I'll be in town for another week or so. But you be sure to call me, aight? And look me up when you get back to Brooklyn," she told him as she looked up into his eyes. He nodded and kissed her lips. Chante looked at me. "Bye, Kia. I'll return your clothes before I leave." I waved it off.

"Don't even worry about it."

"Oh, thanks," she said with a smile. I nodded. She looked up at David again. "Walk me to my car?"

He followed her outside.

I got dressed in jeans and a tank top. Then I picked up the phone to make a call before I left.

"Ay Lacy, wassup, girl?" I said into the receiver.

"Nothin'. How you doin'?"

"Good, good. How's it in the shop today? Busy?"

"The usual, but it'll prob'ly pick up around lunchtime. You know how it is."

"Candice workin' today?" I asked.

"Yeah. Why? You need us to pencil you in?" I laughed.

"Yes, please. This weave is just about through. But I only have like a four-hour window. I need to be at the studio at twelve-thirty."

"Alright. I'm sure that won't be a problem. You know Candice works quickly." I smiled.

"That's what I like to hear. I'm on my way in right now." I hung up and clipped my hair up, throwin' on a blue LA Dodgers baseball cap. "Bye, David!" I shouted as I ran down the stairs.

"Lata!" he called back from his room.

My girl Candice was the only person I liked to do my hair. She owned a shop downtown. She *always* hooked me up and she always worked fast. That was definitely needed with the way my schedule was pickin' up.

I greeted all the familiar faces when I walked inside the shop.

"Hey, girl!" Candice called cheerfully when she saw me. She grinned that big, toothy smile. Her long shiny black hair was pulled up into a ponytail. Her honey-colored skin glowed. I smiled back at her and gave her a hug. Then I rubbed her pregnant belly.

"How's everything goin'?" I asked.

"Same ol', same ol'."

"You 'bout six months along now, huh?"

"Yeah, and we just found out the sex." I grinned at her. "It's a girl."

"Oh!" I exclaimed. I embraced her again. "Congratulations!"

"Oh, thank you."

"We gon' have to throw a shower for you soon." She nodded.

"How you been, though?" she asked as I sat in her chair. I looked at her reflection in the mirror.

"Straight. You know, just workin' a lot. We start promoting my first album in a few weeks, so the schedule's gettin' a little hectic. We on the grind with recording."

"Oh, for real?"

"Yeah. I gotta be at the label for a meeting in a little while, then I'ma be working on dance. And tomorrow I gotta be at the studio all day too." She grinned

"So my girl's really doin' it. Becomin' a star and shit." I smiled.

"Been a long time comin'."

"Word." She pulled off my cap. "Ooh," she said as she took out the hair claw and ran her fingers through my hair. I cringed. Things were never good when she made that sound.

"It's bad, I know."

"You shouldn't wait so long to come in. I've always told you that."

"Well, I told you, things have been a little crazy."

"What time did you say your meeting was?"

"Twelve-thirty. Think it can be done?"

"You gon' need a wash and deep conditioning. And that's *after* we take out the weave." She grabbed my hand to look at my nails. "And you need a fill. That means toes, too."

"Well, the nails can wait a little while. But my hair is in dire need of some TLC." Candice giggled.

"Ya not lyin'. OK, it can be done. I'll schedule you for the mani and pedi tomorrow. Be sure to come in when you get the chance, OK?" I nodded. "We gon' work it out, though, I promise. We cannot have you lookin' tore up while you promote this album." I laughed.

"That's why I love you, girl. You always take care of me."

"Not a problem, Chunky. You just remember me when you blow up." I nodded with a grin. "So what color were you thinkin'?" she asked.

"Well, actually, I was checkin' your hair out when I came in." She smiled.

"Yeah, pregnancy does wonders for hair."

"I was thinkin' black with some brown highlights around the face." She nodded.

"Aight. Let's do it."

After we were done, my shit was tight—dark with highlights, bangs, and tapered in the front. Candice got skills. I had to give it to her. I handled my business and then went back to the shop to pick up Candice. She'd said earlier that she wanted to come with me when I went to Momma's house.

"Hey," my mother greeted us when we walked through the backdoor. She hugged and kissed both of us. "How's everything goin' along?" she asked Candice of her pregnancy.

"Great. We just found out that we're havin' a baby girl, so things couldn't be better."

"Oh, wow, that is great." Momma looked at me.

"When are *you* gon' settle down and give me some grandba-
bies?" I smiled.

"Oh, Ma, you got a lotta years before that'll happen.
Trust me." She smiled back. "Where's Liyah?"

"Downstairs watchin' TV."

"Come on," I said and gestured for Candice to follow
me to the basement. Liyah stood up when she saw Candice.

"Look at you," she said as they hugged. "You almost
in your third trimester already? God, time flies."

"I know it," Candice said.

We all sat on the couch and chatted until David's
footsteps interrupted us. He came down the stairs wearing
jeans, a wife-beater, and Jordans. He looked at me first.

"I like your hair," he said with a grin and an approv-
ing nod. I thanked 'im, and then he looked at Candice warily
'cuz she was just gazing up at him. I held in a laugh.

"Oh," I said, "this is Candice from my old dance
class. Remember?"

"Oh, yeah," he said as he nodded again. He shook
her hand and smiled. "How you doin'?"

"Good, thank you," she said.

"David!" Momma called from the top of the stairwell.

"Yes?" he called back.

"Can you come up here and help me for a second,
please?" He looked at us.

"I'll be right back," he said as he ran up the stairs.
Candice looked at me.

"Has he always been that . . ."

"Sexy?" I asked.

"Gorgeous?" Liyah added. I smiled.

"Fine as hell?"

"Ooh, all of the above," Candice said and we laughed. "Wow, I don't know why I never noticed *him* back in the
day."

"He seems to get more handsome by the day," I
commented.

"Speakin' of fine men," Liyah said, "what happened
with that dude thatchu met at the club?" I smiled.

"Oh, Terrance? Me and him went out last night."

"Oh for real? Where'd he take you?"

"To a play in the city."

"Uh-oh," Candice said. "Chunky's got herself a cultured man, huh."

"I don't know if I would say all that, but it was nice to do somethin' a little different on a date."

"So, how'd it go?" Liyah asked. I smiled again.

"He was so sweet. We didn't even have sex."

"What?!" Candice exclaimed in shock. "And you look like you're OK with that." I nodded.

"I am, for once in my life. We planned to go out again. And I think I might actually hold out with this one." Liyah started chokin' on the soda she was drinkin'. "Damn, are you OK?" I asked. She held up a finger to catch her breath.

"There *must* be somethin' in my ears 'cuz I don't think I heard you right." I furrowed my brow.

"No, you heard me right. Why is everyone actin' like this is so strange? I'm not some hootchie who just sleeps with any and every-damn-body."

"Hold up," Liyah said. "No one said all that, Kia. We're all just surprised that you, *you*, the woman whose time is too precious for a man, actually seems to like someone enough to hold out."

"Well, believe it," I said and stood up.

"Where you goin'?"

"Upstairs to help Momma." She stood up too.

"OK, wait a minute. Don't go throwin' a tantrum now, Chunky. We didn't mean to offend you." I glared at her.

"No one's throwin' a tantrum." Candice tugged on my hand.

"We didn't mean to hurt your feelings," she said, "and we're sorry if we did." I nodded.

"I just wish that for once everyone would give me some credit and stop treating me like 'Little Chunky' because in case you haven't noticed, I am now a woman who is very much capable of carryin' on a relationship. I choose to do what I do and I shouldn't be looked down upon because of it." I looked at Liyah who was standing in my path. "Excuse me."

She shook her head, but sat down so I could leave. David noticed my expression when I walked up to the kitchen.

"What's wrong with you?" he asked. I shook my head as I sat down at the kitchen table. "You sure?" I nodded.

But the truth was that I was tired of getting questioned about why I chose not to be in a relationship. And I was damn sure tired of double standards. What everyone was saying did upset me, but it also made me think. Maybe it was time to slow down.

CHAPTER 4

Kia

Little did I know how easy it would be to stick to that decision. The next month or so had me all booked up. Between recording, time for family, and teaching at the dance studio, I didn't really have *time* to see anyone other than Terrance. Not that I didn't like it that way.

"Wassup, Corri?" I called as I walked into the dance studio. She tucked her blond hair behind her ear and looked up at me with her blue eyes.

"Hey, girl," she responded from behind her desk. "Happy Birthday," she added with a smile. I grinned.

"Oh, thank you."

"Doin' anything special?" I shrugged.

"I haven't planned anything. But maybe my family has a few surprises in store."

"I'm sure they do."

"Paychecks here?" She nodded and handed me mine. "Thanks." She nodded again and I tucked it into my dance bag. I went to the dressing rooms and set my bag down. I changed out of my jeans, sandals, and lacy blouse, and I put on black sweatpants and an old, yellow tee. Then I slipped on some sneakers and put my hair up into a bun.

"Hey y'all," I said when I walked into the room. The girls and guys in this class ranged from thirteen to eighteen. They all greeted me. My girl Jaynie walked in then. Me and her usually taught this particular group together. She was also my choreographer. We hugged each other. "Everyone's here."

She nodded and walked over to the stereo.

"Let's get started then," she said.

"Oh no," I said as I watched the class dance a half hour later. I gestured at Jaynie to stop the music. I called my little cousin Tasha out on the floor. Her thin frame stepped in front of the class nervously. She pulled her braids up into a ponytail and looked up at me attentively. She was thirteen and a little unsure of herself. It sometimes showed in her dancing. We were dancing to Sean Paul's "Gimme the Light" remix and I could see that some of the moves were hard for her to get.

"OK," I said, "I know I usually say you gotta stick all the moves, make things a little rigid. But this is a different style of dance, feel me? With reggae, the moves are sexy," I explained. "They're fluid." I shook her by the shoulders. "And you, miss thang, have got to loosen up." I smiled and she giggled. "OK, watch me. Go 'head, Jaynie."

She turned the music back on. I danced, walking up toward the mirror, then stepping out to drop low, then I wind my waist all the way up to standing. Some of the boys in the class started making catcalls.

"Cut it out, you guys!" Jaynie called. They shut up, but I could tell that they were holding in laughs.

I smiled and looked back at Tasha.

"Alright. Now do it with me." I counted us in. She did the moves with me. She was still a little stiff, but she was getting better. I made her do it by herself with the music. "Aight, aight," I said, "you're gettin' it. Let's move on."

Corri walked up to the doorway then, and Jaynie cut off the track.

"Sorry to interrupt," she called into the studio, "but there's a man here to see you, Kia." I pointed at my chest.

"There's someone here to see *me*?" I asked. "Are you sure?" She nodded with a smile. I started to walk out. I thought it was David at first, but immediately ruled that out.

He'd been to this dance studio so many times that he wouldn't have waited in the lobby. He would've just come right in and made his presence known.

I walked out and grinned when I saw Terrance standing there with two dozen red roses in his hands.

"Oh my god," I said. I pecked him on the lips after he handed them to me. "What're you doing here?" I asked. "How'd you even know I was here?" He smiled.

"I went to your place and David told me you were here. Gave me directions and everything. You didn't think I'd forget your birthday, did you?" I put the flowers on the desk and put my arms around him.

"You are so sweet. Thank you."

"You're welcome," he said as he hugged me back. We kissed before he pulled away completely.

"Whooooooh," I could hear my class sing from behind me. They were watching the whole scene.

I giggled and then shot them a look so they'd stop. I looked up at Terrance.

"I gotta get back," I told him as I gestured with my thumb. "But I'll call you later, OK?"

He nodded and then leaned in to kiss me one last time.

"Bye," he said with a grin. I beamed as I nodded.

"OK, everyone," I said when I turned back around. "Back to work." I ushered them back inside the room.

"Who was that cutie?" Jaynie asked quietly before we started up again. I smiled again.

"Tell you later."

David

"Check you out," I said to Kia when she walked through the front door. She had the roses that Terrance got for her in her hands. She smiled at me as she dropped her keys on the table. "You're like glowing," I told her in my best California accent.

"Shut up. Come help me," she said as she giggled. I

followed her into the kitchen. She pointed on top of the fridge as she put the roses down on the counter. "Grab those vases for me?"

I got the two heavy crystals vases for her and placed them by the sink.

"So it's getting serious between you and this guy, huh," I commented. She smiled again as she filled both vases with water.

"I don't know. I guess," she said with a shrug.

"You guess? The guy bought you two dozen roses and you didn't even give him any. I haven't seen you go out with any other guys in a while either. And didn't y'all exchange keys a few days ago? I'd say that's pretty damn serious."

She looked up at me and nodded her head.

"Or it's getting there at least. I mean, we haven't really talked about commitment or anything." She filled each vase with roses and grabbed one of them. I picked up the other as we walked into the living room. We placed them on opposite ends of the room. "I don't wanna get my hopes up. And I don't want to force things," she told me. I smiled.

"Butchu like him a lot, don'tchu." She smiled and nodded as she sat down on the couch. I sat down next to her and nodded to myself. "So anyway, listen," I said as I began to change the subject, "remember when I asked you to go with me to that dinner a few weeks ago?" She nodded again. "Well, it's tonight. You still wanna go with me?"

"Yeah," she said. "Why wouldn't I?" I shrugged.

"I don't know. You have a boyfriend now," I stated with a smile. "I don't want to make anybody jealous."

"I'm sure it won't be a problem. But it's a formal dinner, right?" I nodded.

"Yeah. Why?"

"'Cuz I don't have a dress."

"Oh," I said, "don't even worry about that. I gotchu." She smiled at me.

"That is really sweet, but you don't have to do that."

"It's not a problem, really. Ever since this album

started climbing the charts, I been makin' more money than I know what to do with. So it's just been stackin' up. I haven't had any real fun with it. You my girl, Chunky. Who better to spend this money on? Plus, it *is* your birthday. I wanna get-chu somethin'." She looked uncertain.

"You sure?" I nodded. "OK," she said as she stood up and tugged on my hand. "Come on then." I chuckled and looked at the clock.

"What, now? It's only two o'clock. Dinner's not 'til eight."

"You've never been shopping with a woman, have you?" I laughed again and shook my head. "Trust me, David, finding the right dress is gonna take a while." She grabbed her keys as she led the way out the front door.

"I'll drive," I announced as I locked the door behind me.

I don't know what Kia expected when I told her that I wanted to spend some money on her, but I was sure she didn't expect me to drive up Rodeo Drive. She looked at me curiously when I pulled up in front of Dolce & Gabbana. I just smiled as I stepped out of the car.

"David," she said as she got out, "when I said let's go find a dress, I just meant let's go to the mall or something. Dolce Gabbana? Do you know how much these dresses cost?" I nodded. "And you're willing to spend that much on *me*?" I smiled and nodded again. She grinned. "You're crazy."

"I know this." She was still hesitant, so I started to walk back over to the driver's side of my car. "But if you don't wanna shop here, we can still go to the mall," I said. She grabbed my hand.

"Oh no," she contested. "I'm takin' full advantage of your insanity right now. Who knows when it'll happen again?"

I chuckled and we walked into the store.

I was a little apprehensive when we stepped in be-cause of the way we were stared at by customers and some of the sales people. But I figured it was to be expected. Two young black people in jeans in a high-end store on Rodeo Drive, and it was bound to happen, so I got over that quickly. They didn't know shit about us. We were here to shop just like everyone else. Kia grabbed my hand again as we walked over to the service desk; I guess she was uneasy too. The lady at the desk looked friendly, though. And when I say friendly, I mean black and pretty young herself.

"Hi," she said with a bright smile. "How can I help you?" I smiled back.

"We're going to a formal dinner tonight, and she"—I gestured at Kia—"needs a dress." She looked at Kia.

"Were you thinking of something in particular?" she asked.

Chunky let go of my hand and shrugged.

"Just something elegant."

"OK, let's see what we can find." She stepped out from behind the desk. "What size are you?"

"Eight," Kia said.

The saleswoman's name was Kelly. She led us around the store, showing us various styles. Kia would always look at me for approval and I would say yes or no to each of them. By the time she went into the dressing room, she had about twelve dresses or more to try on. I sat down. Kelly looked at me then.

"This is gonna sound like some kind of line," she said with a smile, "but don't I know you from somewhere?"

I shook my head as I smiled back.

"I don't think so."

"No, I'm positive I've seen your face before." I shrugged.

"I don't think so," I repeated, "unless you're into rap music, that is." She snapped her fingers.

"That's it. You're BK, right? The rapper?" I nodded. "My son loves your album. I swear it's the only thing he plays." I smiled.

"How old is he?"

"Fourteen. Actually, hold on one second." She disappeared toward the back, and came back a moment later with one of my CDs in her hands. She grabbed a Sharpie off the desk in front of us. "Can you sign an autograph for him, please? He'll never believe I saw you if you don't." I laughed.

"Sure," I said as I grabbed the pen and signed.

"Thank you. He'll love this." I smiled again.

"No problem."

Kia came out then and modeled a blue dress for me. She smiled and spun around.

"What do you think?" she asked.

"It's pretty," I told her. And it was. It was made of a silky material, but I didn't think it suited her.

"But not me, huh?" she said, reading my mind. I shook my head. She smiled again and said, "OK, I'll be back." She ducked back into the dressing room.

"Your girlfriend is really beautiful," Kelly commented.

I grinned but didn't correct her assumption.

"I know."

We were about ten dresses deep when I started to realize what she meant by "finding the right dress is gonna take a while." I have to admit, though, I was having fun. And most importantly, Kia was having a ball. She looked gorgeous in every single dress she tried on, but it was when she came out in this light pink dress that I really took notice. It had one strap that went across to her right shoulder. There was a split that went up to her hip where the material was held together by lace. When she turned, I saw that the back was cut real low.

"Wow," I said when she turned back around. I stood up. She grinned.

"You like this one?" I nodded.

"Yeah."

"You sure?"

"Oh, yeah," I said.

"You don't think it's too sexy?" I shook my head.

"No, not at all. It's perfect." She was beaming from ear-to-ear.

"Really? I kinda liked that black one I had on." I smiled back at her.

"You can pick whatchu want. Either way, I'm buyin' *this* dress for you. It makes no difference to me." She giggled.

"You really *are* insane."

"No, *you're* insane if you don't pick this one." She laughed again.

"OK, this one it is."

She went back into the dressing room and came back out a few moments later in her blouse and jeans. I stretched as I got my wallet out, ready to pay for the dress.

"What're you doing?" Kia asked.

"Paying for it," I replied.

"Oh, we're not done yet." I raised my eyebrows.

"We're not?"

She shook her head with a smile.

"You cannot buy a dress without shoes, David," she said. She handed the dress to Kelly. "Can you hold this behind the counter for me?"

Kelly nodded with a grin as Kia grabbed my hand and pulled me to a different section of the store.

"Come on."

"Oh man," I said. "What have I got myself into?" Kia just laughed.

Later on that evening I was dressed in my tux when I went up to Kia's bedroom door and knocked.

"Come in," she called. I opened the door. She stood there in her dress and shoes in front of her dresser mirror. Candice had done her hair and makeup. She smiled at me. "Almost ready," she said. I nodded.

"Can I talk to you in private for a sec?" I asked. Candice smiled.

"I'll just be downstairs," she told Kia.

"What's up?" she asked. I smiled.

"I have something for you."

"You what? There's more? The dress and shoes are enough." I shook my head.

"No, they're not," I said. "Not hardly." I took out what I'd been hiding behind my back—a long, velvet box.

She looked at me curiously as I opened it. A diamond necklace sparkled back at us.

"Oh my god," she uttered as she placed her hand on her chest. She looked into my eyes. "You shouldn't have." I took the necklace and clipped it around her neck. "You *really* shouldn't have," she said as she noticed it shine in the mirror. She looked up at my reflection. "Why are you doin' all this?" she wanted to know.

"'Cuz, you have been my girl forever, but I don't think I've ever really told you how much you mean to me. Besides my mother, you are the most important woman in the world to me and I wanted to let you know. And now that I am making money, I just want to give you everything you deserve." I shrugged. "Make up for lost time, so to speak."

Tears welled up in her eyes when she smiled at me. I grabbed a tissue off the dresser and handed it to her.

"Dammit, David, you're gonna make me mess up my makeup," she joked with a laugh. She patted her eyes and then turned to look at me. "Thank you."

"You're welcome," I said as I pulled her into my arms. "Happy Birthday, Chunky."

"Thanks."

"And in case I forgot to tell you today, you look absolutely beautiful."

"Thank you," she said again. She pulled away as a black tear rolled down her cheek. Her makeup *was* starting to run. "OK, enough, enough." She wiped her tears and looked in the mirror. "See the mess you made?" she teased. I laughed as I headed for the door.

"I'll call Candice up to fix it."

The front door unlocked just as Candice went back upstairs. Terrance walked in with Kareem behind him. I gave both of them dap.

"Where is she?" Terrance asked. He'd come over to see Kia in her new dress. I smiled.

"Upstairs fixing her makeup. She'll be down in a

second." Kareem looked at his watch.

"I guess we can be a little bit late," he said. I grinned and patted his shoulder.

"Trust me, it's worth it."

Kia came down a moment later and the guys' reactions were priceless.

"Oh my god," Terrance said as he walked over to her.

I looked at Kareem and smiled. His mouth was wide open.

"Pick your jaw up off the floor, dawg," I told him. He looked at me. "Told you it would be worth it."

Kia

"What was that all about?" Candice asked when she came back up into my room. "Why you cryin'?"

I held up my necklace to show her.

"This," I said.

"Wow," she said as she came over to look at it. "Damn, he just went all out for your birthday, huh." I nodded.

"And all the stuff he was sayin' just made me tear up." She gestured for me sit on the bed.

"Like what?" she asked as she attempted to fix my face.

"Like how I'm one of the most important women in his life and he wants to give me everything I deserve."

"What?" Candice said. "If I didn't know any better, I would think that he was in love with you or something."

"You think?"

"I don't know. You know him better than I do. What do you think?"

"It would explain all this sudden affection. Maybe he was just using my birthday as an excuse."

"Maybe." She stepped back and looked at me with a smile. "You're all done." I smiled back, stood up, and hugged her.

"Thank you, girl."

"No problem."

"Come on, I'm already late," I said as I grabbed my purse and headed out the door. I walked into the living room and smiled at everyone. Kareem just about lost it. Terrance smiled at me.

"Oh my god," he said as he came up to me. He grabbed my hand and pulled me into the kitchen. "You look so good," he told me when we got there. I smiled.

"Thank you."

He looked at me with a sexy grin and slid his arms around my waist. He kissed my lips softly.

"I'm sayin' though, do you *have* to go to this dinner?" I giggled. "We can easily just go back to my place."

"You don't know how tempting that offer sounds." He kissed my lips again. "Tell you what, after it's over, I'll definitely come see you."

"I'ma hold you to that," he said. "Call me as soon as you're done." I grinned. "I'm serious. I'll be waiting up." I smiled again.

"I will."

I called Terrance at quarter of two while Kareem was driving us home.

"Hey," I said with a smile when I heard his voice. "You still awake?"

"I'm doin' my best," he told me sleepily. "You still comin' over, right?"

"Of course."

"Can't wait to see you." I smiled again.

"Me too."

"OK. See you in a few."

"Bye."

Kareem dropped me off in front of Terrance's apartment about a half-hour later. I unlocked the door and stepped inside. The soft glow of the TV was the only light in the place. Terrance had dozed off on the couch in a wife-beater and boxer shorts. I took off my shoes and put down my purse. I walked over to the couch and sat down. I stroked his cheek before I leaned in and kissed his lips.

"Mmm," he moaned as he kissed back. We smiled at each other when I pulled away. "Now that's how a man likes to be woken up," he said with a grin. "So how was it? Did you have fun?"

"Yeah, I did."

"Betchu had plenny of guys tryna talk to you, too." I smiled again.

"No, not really."

He sat up and chuckled.

"Yeah, right. As sexy as you look in that dress?" I placed my hand over my chest.

"I swear. Why you wanna know anyway? Were you worried?" He shook his head.

"Of course not. I knew you were comin' back to me at the end of the night."

"Oh, you're just that sure of yourself, huh?" He just smiled and kissed me again. "So I suppose you're too tired to do anything now." He laughed.

"You underestimate me. Girl, I been waitin' to getchu outta that dress all night." I grinned.

"Really?" I stood up and slipped outta the dress. He smiled as he watched it drop to the floor and reveal my naked body. He stood up and took off his wife-beater. I smiled as I slid my hands over his pecs. He kissed me deeply as he stroked my body. He laid me down on the couch and kissed my neck. I sighed as he moved down my chest, stomach, and then he teased me by kissing and licking my hips. I moaned when he put one of my breasts in his mouth and licked around the nipple. He reached over me and grabbed a condom off the end table. I couldn't help but laugh.

"So you weren't even gonna take me to the bedroom?" I asked with a smile. He grinned.

"Told you I been waitin' for this all night. I wanted to be prepared for every scenario."

I laughed again. He kissed my lips as I used my feet to push down his boxers. He opened the condom wrapper and slid it on. He put my right leg up over his shoulder, and then he pumped hard, making me cry out. I was loving every minute of it. He stood up and slipped out of his boxers all the way, and then he put both my legs over his shoulders. My hips were raised as he started thrusting again.

"Ooh yesss," I sighed. "Harder, baby." He slammed his hips into me. "Harder," I commanded again. He moved harder and faster until my body shook under his weight. He made me scream for more. I was begging for him not to stop.

He lay on top of me on the couch when it was over. Neither of us had enough strength to actually go to bed, so we just fell asleep there. He'd hit it right.

"Hey," I said to Liyah and 'Ren as I met up with them for lunch the next day.

They both greeted me when I sat down. I had on a tank top and jeans, so my new diamond necklace was very visible. Karen reached over and grabbed my necklace before any other words were spoken.

"Who gave you this?" she asked as she inspected it. I grinned.

"David."

"What?" Liyah said as 'Ren sat back down. "Lemme see." She stood up to check it out as well. "With a dress *and* shoes?" she asked as she sat back down. "Damn, you put him under one helluva spell." I shrugged.

"I haven't done anything. He told me he was just makin' up for lost time, since he'd never really told me how much I meant to him. Candice thinks he might have feelings for me."

"I think Candice is right," Karen said just as the waitress walked over. Our conversation was briefly interrupted as the waitress took our orders. "I told you he would see, Kia," she finished with a smile.

"Personally, I think he's always seen," Liyah added.

"What do you mean?" I asked.

"You've always been David's number one, didn't you know that?"

I shook my head.

"No. He's never said anything to me."

"Well, you've never been one for relationships and he's like the serial monogamist. He prob'ly thought it wouldn't work." I shook my head again.

"I think you guys are wrong. Me and him talk about everything. I'm sure he would've told me if his feelings were more than platonic. And for the last time, I'm not against relationships. If the right guy came along, I would definitely be open."

"Maybe he doesn't know that," Karen said.

"Speaking of that," Liyah said, switching gears a bit, "Candice told me about the roses you got," she informed me with a smile.

"What roses?" Karen asked. I grinned.

"Yesterday Terrance came to the dance studio and surprised me with two dozen roses."

"Aww," Karen cooed, "that's so sweet."

"He is sweet," I gushed. I smiled again. "Last night," I started quietly, "we had sex for the first time and it was sooo good."

"Really?" Liyah asked. I nodded. "You really like him, huh." I nodded.

"I do."

"Does he feel that way about you?" 'Ren asked. I shrugged.

"I don't know. I think so."

"Have y'all talked about not seein' other people?" Liyah asked. I shook my head.

"I'm afraid to."

"Why? You said you were open," 'Ren said.

"Oh, I am," I replied. "It's not that. I just don't wanna scare him off, ya know? I think the fact that I am so relaxed about relationships is one of the reasons he likes me."

"You should talk to him," Liyah told me.

"Wouldn't that kinda force the issue?" I asked.

"It doesn't have to be like an ultimatum—commit to me or die—or anything." I laughed "You can just get your feelings out there. At least he'll know."

I thought about it as the food came and then smiled.

"Maybe I will talk to him," I said.

I opened the door to Terrance's apartment a few days later and went into the kitchen to set down my groceries. I had decided to tell Terrance how I felt. Liyah and 'Ren were right. Even if he didn't feel the same way right now, I could at least get my feelings out on the table.

I dropped my keys on the counter and slipped out of my flip-flops. I started putting things away and that's when I heard it—a woman's giggle followed by Terrance's voice. It was coming from his bedroom.

I walked up to the doorway and quietly pushed open the door. They were so busy that they didn't even notice me. She was on top of him, riding him, and he was moaning in ecstasy. The sheets didn't even cover their bodies. I could see everything. I gasped as my breath caught in my throat. A tear fell from my eye. Terrance sat up and that's when he noticed me standing in his bedroom doorway.

"Kia?" he said with a shocked expression on his face.

I snapped out of my own shock and started back down the hallway. I could hear him scrambling to follow me. I slid my feet back into my sandals and grabbed my keys as he walked up the hallway in a pair of boxers. I didn't say anything to him as I moved to grab my purse. He grasped my hand. I looked into his eyes, pulled away, and crossed my arms.

"You really shouldn't have other women over here when there's another woman who has a key," I told him pointedly. I started to take his key off my key ring.

"Well, you usually call before you come over," he retorted. I shook my head.

"Unbelievable." He looked confused.

"You can't possibly be mad at me," he said. "We never once talked about commitment." I nodded and looked down.

"You're right. We never did." I looked back into his face. "I was gonna do it tonight." I gestured at the grocery bags in the kitchen. "I was gonna cook dinner and there was wine. . . . I was gonna tell you that I wanted to be with you, the first guy that I've *ever* had feelings for." Another tear fell from my cheek. "I haven't seen anyone other than you in weeks, Terrance. And for me that's damn sure a stretch." I looked away from him. "God, I am such an idiot."

"You are not an idiot," he said as he grabbed my hand again. I smiled a little.

"Yeah, I am, because for some reason I actually thought that we might've been on the same page." I pulled my hand away and placed the key in his palm. He looked into my eyes. It was obvious to me that he felt bad, but the feelings I had for him were not mutual. "I guess I was wrong."

"Kia, I care about you a lot, but—" I put up a hand.

"Don't. Please, just don't." I grabbed my purse.

"What about your groceries?" he asked before I could leave. I exhaled, annoyed.

"Just keep 'em, Terrance, alright? Enjoy."

He nodded and I walked out.

David

Kia stormed in the front door. She jumped when she saw me and I noticed that tears streaked her cheeks. She quickly turned away from my alarmed eyes and wiped them away. I stood up.

"I didn't think you'd be home," she said.

"I finished rehearsal early," I explained. "Why you cryin'? What happened?"

"Nothing," she said with a shake of her head. She looked down at the floor. I took her chin into my hands and moved her head to look up at me. More tears streamed out of her eyes before she could stop them, so I put my arms around her.

"It's obviously not nothing," I said. I wiped her cheeks as she looked up at me again. She pulled away and stepped behind me.

"This is so stupid. I don't cry over guys." I turned to look at her.

"This is about Terrance? What'd he do?" She crossed her arms angrily.

"Doesn't matter."

"Kia, this is me, aight?" I put my hand on my chest. "You don't have to put a wall up with me. You like the guy. There's nothing wrong with that. And there's nothing wrong with being hurt by whatever he's done either." I grabbed her hands and sat her down on the couch with me. "Please talk to me."

She took a deep breath before she spoke.

"I caught him in bed with another girl." I raised my eyebrows. "That's not the worst part."

"What's the worst part?" I asked.

"I'd gone over there to cook for him and tell him that I wanted to be with him, just him."

"Whoa," I said in amazement. "Really?" She nodded. "I didn't know you liked him *that* much." She nodded again.

"I did. But I was so stupid to think that he felt the same way. This is why I don't let any guys in. They always hurtchu."

"I don't believe that for a second. I don't believe whatchu felt was stupid either. Actually, I'm kinda glad to see that you were able to bring your wall down. I used to wonder if you were even capable. I'm sayin', how are you supposed to feel anything if you keep shutting people out?"

"It's painful to let people in."

"But if you don't, you might miss out on someone who could be perfect for you, you know?"

"Yeah."

"Why do you shut men out like this? I never understood that."

She shrugged. "I don't know. I guess, after watching my mother chase Daddy around with all those women when I was younger, and seeing the way he kept hurting her, I swore I would never let it happen to me."

"Man, I know some people put their guard up, but you?"—I smiled—"You have an electric fence with pitbulls and shit around your heart."

Kia smiled slightly. "I can't help it." She exhaled as she looked at the clock and wiped her face. "Geez, I'm s'posed to be goin' to this label party tonight and I don't know if I feel like it. Now I don't even have anyone to go with."

"Oh, so I guess I just don't count, huh?" I joked with her. She smiled.

"You wanna come with me?"

"I don't know," I responded, crossing my arms. "I don't know if I feel like it anymore," I teased as I looked away.

She grabbed onto my arm and rested her chin on my shoulder.

"Please?" She pouted. "Pleeeease, David?"

"Not if you don't want me to," I told her with a smile, still playin'. She grinned.

"I want you to. Puh-leeese come with me," she pleaded. I nodded.

"Aight, I'll go." I pinched her cheek. "Who could resist those eyes and this face?"

She smiled again and kissed me on the cheek.

"Thank you." She reached over me and grabbed the phone. "I'm gonna call and check on the arrangements right now."

PART TWO:

A MISUNDERSTANDING

PILOT PUBLISHING

CHAPTER 5

Kia

After that whole situation with Terrance, I just worked on my music and tried to forget about him. I damn sure was focused. If I wasn't at the studio, I was dancing. If I wasn't dancing, I was doin' press, and so on and so on. For a while, David and I became like two trains passing in the night. We rarely saw each other because he was promoting his album too.

Jaynie counted me off one day when I was in the dance studio practicing a routine for an upcoming video shoot. This was about the hundredth time we'd gone over the routine that day. I thought I had it down, but Jaynie was relentless, so over and over again I practiced until, I spun, heard a pop, and then collapsed in pain.

"Oh my god!" Jaynie exclaimed. "What is it? Are you OK?" I cringed.

"It's my ankle."

"I'm so sorry. I shouldn't have been pushing so hard. Can you walk?"

I tried to get up, but sat back down when the pain became unbearable.

"No, I can't. It hurts too much," I said.

Jaynie helped me stand on my good foot.

"Come on. We have to get you to a hospital."

The doctor who examined my ankle said that it was a mild fracture, but I would have to wear a cast and use crutches for a month.

"You've got to be kidding me," I said. "I'm a performer. I can't just sit on my butt for a month."

She smiled with empathy showing in her eyes.

"I'm sorry. I wish I had better news for you." I nodded glumly. She patted my knee. "I'll be back to make the cast."

She walked out and Jaynie immediately started apologizing again.

"Don't worry about it. Accidents happen," I told her. "Can you pass me my purse?" She did and I checked my phone. *Five missed calls? Who the hell is trying to get in touch with me?* I wondered. My phone rang before I could check the numbers and call anyone back. "Hello?" I answered.

"Hey, what's up?" David asked. "Candice just called here for you."

"Oh, is that who keeps calling me?"

"Yeah, she's at the hospital. The baby's coming."

"Oh what!!" I exclaimed. I was so excited that I almost hopped down off the table, broken ankle and all. Jaynie looked at me.

"What's going on?" she asked quietly. I put up my index finger.

"No wonder she's been blowing up my phone." David laughed.

"Yeah, you need to get to the hospital right away." I giggled.

"I don't think that'll be a problem."

"Why's that?" he asked curiously. I laughed again.

"Because I'm already here."

"What? Are you alright?"

"Yeah, I kinda had an accident at dance rehearsal. Short version—I'll be out of commission for about a month because of the cast on my foot."

"What?" David said again.

"I know. But listen, the doctor will be back in a few. I wanna call Candice before she comes back."

"Can I come see you, though?" David asked. I smiled. He sounded worried.

"That's sweet. But it's really not that bad, I promise."

"I'm gonna come anyway. Besides, we live together, but I feel like I haven't really seen you since we went to that party—"

"Almost three months ago," I finished with another smile.

"I'll be there in like fifteen minutes."

"OK, I'll be here."

"I guess it's good thing I got some time off, huh," he said when he arrived.

"Why's that?" I asked as he helped me down off the table.

"'Cuz, you gon' need help with everything. Going to the grocery store, for instance. You can't drive now that your right foot is out of commission." I grabbed my crutches and sighed. I hadn't thought about that.

"This month is going to be hell," I commented. He chuckled at me.

We all walked over to the maternity ward. Everyone was hugging and laughing. Candice had her eight pound, ten ounce baby girl at four PM—Neveah Renee Grant. Momma and baby were both healthy. We were allowed to see Candice a few hours later.

"Hey," I said when Jaynie and I walked into Candice's hospital room. She smiled at both of us as we walked over to her bedside. She glanced at my crutches.

"What happened to you?" she asked. I waved it off as I sat down.

"Just a little mishap during rehearsal. Gotta keep this thing on for a month. How are you feeling?" She smiled again.

"Still a little groggy, but other than that, I couldn't be happier. Have you seen her?"

"Yeah," Jaynie answered. "She's beautiful, girl."

"I know. She looks just like her mommy." She batted her eyelashes and we all giggled.

"How's it feel to be a 'mommy'," I asked.

"A little scary. I mean, that little person's life is in my

hands now, ya know?" Jaynie and I nodded.

"How was Jared during labor?" Jaynie wanted to know.

"All men are punks!" Candice exclaimed, making us crack up again.

"Yeah, girl," I agreed. "That's why we have the babies."

The door opened just then and Karen poked her head through. We all could see the redness in her eyes before she walked across the room.

"Uh-oh," Candice said. "Here comes drama."

"Hey, y'all," 'Ren said as she stepped closer to us. She looked at me first. "What happened?" she inquired, pointing at my foot. I shrugged.

"Broken ankle, dance rehearsal. What's wrong with you?" She avoided the question.

"Shouldn't we be focused on Candice?"

"Uh-uh, girl," Candice spoke up. "I'm fine. The baby's fine, so there's nothing else to talk about." She patted a spot next to her on the bed. "Now tell us what happened." 'Ren gently rested her head on Candice's chest.

"Tony broke up with me," she told us. I shook my head.

"I knew it," I said. "I knew that man was gonna break your heart." 'Ren sat up again.

"Don't start with that stuff, Kia. It wasn't like that. He just decided that it was time for him to be with his kids. He and his ex are gonna try to be a family again."

"Hmph," Jaynie grunted. "Sounds to me like you're better off without him."

"Finally someone agrees with me," I said

"How can you say that?" Karen exclaimed defensively. "You guys barely even knew him."

"How can you *not* say it, 'Ren?" I argued.

"He *did* just break it off," Jaynie added.

'Ren looked at Candice for help. She shrugged.

"I'm sorry, sweetie, but I agree with them. All he ever seemed to do was hurt you. I just never said anything 'cuz I felt like it was none of my business." Karen glared at all of us.

"So all of y'all are against me?"

"No, just the opposite," I contested. "We just want you to be happy. Tony didn't do that for you."

"Actually, he was everything to me," 'Ren said as she stood up. "Nice to know all of you were rooting for us to fail." She walked out, leaving all of us at a loss for words.

During the next two weeks I was trying to adjust to being crippled, but hobbling around with crutches was driving me nuts. David would often scold me about not using them. But my hard-headed ass was just not listening.

One day I slipped while coming out of the shower.

"Ow!" I yelled, but my pride was bruised more than anything else. I started laughing. "Oh shit," I said to myself. There was a knock on the door.

"You OK?" David asked through the door.

"I'm good," I called back.

"Are you sure?" He started to open the door.

"David!" I shouted and kicked the door closed with my left foot. "I'm naked in here." I could hear him laughing. Then there was a pause. *Oh shit*, I thought, *he spotted the crutches.*

"You in there without your crutches? Are you crazy? You could've hurt yourself worse."

"You worry too much. I'm OK, really." There was another pause.

"Grab a towel. I'm comin' in," he told me.

I quickly pulled a towel down over me and made sure it covered everything. He opened the door. His eyes were closed. He opened up one eye after a second. I smiled up at him and he smiled back.

"I don't know why you insist on not using your crutches and then not wanting help." He grabbed one of my hands. "Hold your towel to you," he told me and effortlessly pulled me up. I held onto his shoulder as I wrapped the towel around myself. He looked away, at least at first. I let him get a peek at my butt when I looked up and noticed him glancing down.

"OK," I said. I smiled coyly at his reflection in the bathroom mirror.

He lifted me up in his strong arms. I don't think I ever noticed how good he smelled 'til that moment. I had to admit, it made me a little giddy inside. I put one arm around his neck and used the other to hold the towel. He looked into my eyes.

"You good?" he asked. I nodded.

He smiled a little as he placed me down on my bed.

"What is that smile about?" I asked as if I didn't already know. I knew the image of my ass was still in his head. He shook his head.

"Nothin'." He started to walk out of my room.

"Thank you," I called.

He grinned at me as he turned back.

"You're welcome. Just start using your crutches, aight? Especially after taking a shower." I nodded. "Matter of fact, take bathes until you get your cast off, please. You don't wanna break something else." I smiled back.

"OK, David. Cross my heart." I made an X with my index finger over my chest. I grinned to myself as he walked back downstairs.

David

I opened the door again, but with my eyes closed and this time she didn't stop me. I opened one eye first. She was on the floor with a towel laid over her naked body. I smiled as I looked down at her. "I don't know why you insist on not using your crutches and then not wanting help." I grabbed one of her hands. "Hold your towel to you." I gently pulled her up. I let her hold onto me and looked away as she wrapped the towel around herself. OK, I'm lyin', I may have peeked a little, but I didn't see much. She did it too quick. All I caught was the cute dimple she had on her left butt-cheek.

"OK," she said. She smiled at my reflection in the

mirror.

I picked her up and cradled her in my arms. "You good?" I asked though I knew there was no way I would drop her. She nodded, one arm around my neck and the other held the towel to her chest.

I smiled as I walked into her bedroom and placed her on the bed. "What is that smile about?" She asked suspiciously.

"Nothin'," I said with a shake of my head. I started to walk out.

"Thank you," she called after me.

I smiled again as I turned back. "You're welcome. Just start using your crutches, aight? Especially after taking a shower." She nodded. "Matter of fact, take bathes until you get your cast off please. You don't wanna break something else."

She grinned. "OK, David. Cross my heart." She made the gestured across her chest, like she had done so many times when we were kids. I couldn't get over how cute she looked, though, as she was sat there in just a towel, cast and all. I smiled again as I walked back down the stairs. The phone rang as I stepped off the steps.

"I got it!" I yelled as I jogged over to it. I picked up the cordless. "Hello?"

"Hi, sweetie," I heard my mother say. "How are you?"

"Good. Got a little time off, so I'm relaxin'." I sat down on the couch. "How are things with you?"

"Pretty good. Just tryna get my things moved over to the new place."

"Oh, yeah. I forgot you were doin' that this weekend. How's it comin' along?"

"Slowly. I wish you were here to help me. The movers only do so much, ya know? There's a lot of unpacking to do." I thought.

"Well, maybe I can come up and visit."

"Really?"

"Yeah. I mean, who knows when I'll have time to do

it again. I can spend my last couple of weeks off witcha."

"That sounds great."

"Yeah. I can prob'ly be over there by Sunday morning."

"Oh, that's only a couple of days away, baby. You sure you can make arrangements that quickly?" I chuckled.

"You can be impulsive as you wanna be when you have money." She laughed.

"Good point."

"I'm gonna ask Kia if she wants to come, too. It's been awhile since y'all have seen each other, huh."

"Yeah, 'bout two years or so."

"OK, so I have to make some calls and get things set. I'll call you back later."

"OK, hun."

"Bye."

I hung up and ran back up the steps. Kia's bedroom door was open. She was fully dressed now, wearing a pair of ripped jeans and a tube top while sitting on the bed reading a magazine. I smiled, got a running start, and leapt onto the bed next to her like I used to do when we were younger. I could see her grit her teeth as she turned to look at me. Did I mention that this used to annoy the shit outta her? I grinned. She smiled back slightly.

"I used to hate when you did that," she said. I turned onto my back and looked up at her as she propped herself up on her elbow. "What's up?"

"Come to New York with me," I said bluntly.

"OK," she said slowly in response to my candor. "When?"

"I was thinking Sunday morning."

"Damn, what the hell kind of notice is that?"

"I was talking to my mother and it came to me." I shrugged. "Say yes." She was hesitant.

"I don't know if I wanna go with this cast on my foot."

"Why not?"

"Because we won't have a car over there."

"Oh, yeah, that's right."

"Yes, and I'd rather not be hobbling around Brooklyn."

"Well, it's goin' on three weeks with the cast. Maybe you can talk to your doctor about getting it taken off early." She shook her head.

"I doubt it. That would mean I'd need to get an appointment for tonight or tomorrow morning."

"Is that the only thing stoppin' you from comin'?"

"That, and how long do you plan on stayin' over there?"

"A couple weeks."

"Madd packing to do." I shook my head.

"So many excuses. Make the call to your doctor. And I promise I will help you pack." She was still hesitant. "Just say yes, please? My mom can't wait to see you."

She smiled. I knew that would get her.

"OK, damn," she said. "I'll go."

As it turned out, Kia was able to get a doctor's appointment for the next morning. And after a few X-rays she was told that it would be OK to take the cast off as long as she took it easy.

We set off for New York at around four-thirty AM Sunday morning.

CHAPTER 6

Kia

I made sure to grab my gray hoody and leather jacket before we stepped off the plane that Sunday. It was early March so I knew it would be cold as hell outside, especially to someone who wasn't used to it. That was the only downside to being back in Brooklyn. Other than that, this place was my second home. I knew the streets of BK almost as well as I knew my own and I was glad David had convinced me to go with him.

Miss Pam was excited when we walked into the airport. She looked good—still fairly thin with one of those Halle Berry short haircuts. She shared the same medium-toned skin as David and was wearing a black, puffy coat over a blouse and some jeans. She hugged her son tightly when we walked up to her. I'm sure if it wasn't for the fact that I was standing right next to him, she probably would've looked right over me. She smiled at me with open arms.

"Look at you!" she exclaimed, hugging me. I smiled when she pulled away. "You get prettier and prettier every time I see you, I swear." I blushed.

"Thanks."

"Well," she said, "let's go get your bags and get outta here. You guys must be exhausted after such a long flight."

I woke up from a nap and looked at the clock on the nightstand beside me. Almost five o'clock. *Damn, how long have I been sleeping?* I wondered. The time change had me trippin'. I picked up my watch off the nightstand and checked the time. It was only two o'clock in LA. I had only been asleep for an hour and a half. I grabbed my cell and called my mother to let her know that we'd made it to New York safely.

I pulled off my hoody and took off my socks. Miss Pam had the heat blasting in her place as always. I walked downstairs in a cut-off tank and jeans.

"Wow," Miss Pam said when I walked into the kitchen. She and David were washing dishes and putting things away. "You were right, she *is* tinier than I thought," she said to her son. I giggled as I sat down at the kitchen table.

"You guys were talkin' about me?"

"Yeah. He was telling me how you have your belly button pierced and a tattoo."

I smiled. The tattoo was new. I'd gotten it about a month ago—flames going through my nickname on the small of my back. All my girls had the same one with their nicknames.

"Stand up. Lemme look atchu again," she said. I did and spun around so she could see my tattoo. "I can't get over how small you are. It's like you're a totally different person. I like your tattoo, but I guess we can't really call you Chunky anymore, huh." I shrugged as I sat back down.

"Everyone at home still does. So does David." He smiled at me and I grinned back. "I don't mind." She walked back over to the sink.

"You hungry, sweetie? I haven't had time to cook anything, but we could order something. Or . . ." She looked through some grocery bags by the backdoor. She pulled out a box of Coco Puffs and I smiled again as she put it on the table. She smiled back. "I got this for you yesterday."

"You are the best." She was still grinning.

"I know," she said with a chuckle. "There's milk in the fridge."

David

A snowstorm kept me and Kia in the house for the

first few days. It was cool at first, but cabin fever soon set in and we were excited when we actually got to leave and check out all our old hangouts. Surprisingly, it wasn't that cold either. We hopped the subway and went to my old neighborhood.

We met up with my boy Ray-Ray after walking around and greeting old acquaintances. He'd been my nigga from way back. We lived across the street from each other in high school. That dude was always smoking somethin'. He burned everything from cigarettes to weed. His voice was madd raspy and he had this horrible smoker's cough as a result. Me and Kia used to sneak and smoke trees wit' 'im, though, back in the day. He was puffing on a cherry cigar when we walked up to his stoop. He grinned and stood up.

"What's good, man?" he asked as we gave each other dap and a brief hug. He slowly inhaled his cigar one last time and then flicked the end away. "Heard you were down in Cali again. When'd you get back?"

"A few days ago," I told him. "I woulda holla'ed sooner but that storm had me stuck in the house."

"That's cool." He coughed and then looked at Kia. She smiled at him. She knew he didn't recognize 'er. I grinned too, amused.

"Damn, Ray-Ray," she said with her hands on her hips, "you just gon' stare at me, huh? Say somethin'."

He looked confused and I know he was thinkin', *why is this bitch talkin' to me like she knows me?* Kia shook her head and looked up at me.

"Maybe you should introduce us." I smiled again and gestured at her.

"Ray-Ray, Kia—"

"Whoa," he cut me off and we all laughed. "Wait a minute. Kia?" He stepped off the stoop and looked at her again. She smiled and opened up her jacket. Her clothes were form-fitting and Ray-Ray checked her out. "I can't believe this," he said and smiled again as he hugged her. He looked down at her ass and then at me. *Oh my god*, he mouthed and I chuckled to myself. "How you been, ma?" he asked when they pulled away from each other. "Been a while." She nodded.

"I been straight. Working on my music thing."

"Oh, yeah, I remember you had a sensual-ass voice that I loved." Kia grinned and nodded. "How's that goin'?" She shrugged.

"It's goin'. Gotta finish the album and drop it. It's been fun, though. You know I've always loved recording. You still flow?"

"Of course. I'm still waitin' for this nigga to put me on." He smiled and pointed at me with his thumb. I laughed. "Matter of fact, come in and listen to some of my new shit."

Ray-Ray led us into his building and up a flight of stairs. He unlocked the door to his apartment and let us in. He still had the mic set up behind the couch with his 808 and other newer equipment. He walked over and started searching through a stack of CDs. Kia and I smiled at each other and I knew we were both nostalgic as hell at the sight of Ray-Ray's place. A group of us was always recording here. It drove his grandmother crazy. I could almost hear her yelling for us to turn down the music.

"How's your grandmother?" I asked.

He looked back at us with a smile as we took off our coats and sat down on one of the couches.

"She's good. Stay a while. She should be back soon so you can say hi." He played a couple of tracks for us.

"That was hott, dawg," I said after the last track. He grinned.

"Hott enough for you to talk to Kareem?" I smiled.

"Will it getchu off my back?" He nodded. "Aight, I will as soon as I go back." He stood up.

"Bet." Ray moved to turn off the music, but Kia stopped him.

"Wait a minute. What's that?" The next track was playing and I think my face turned about white as a black man's face could get. She looked up at me. "What's wrong with you?"

I played it off.

"Nothing."

"That beat is crazy," she commented.

"Yeah, this is somethin' me and David did the last time he was here," Ray-Ray said.

I was just waiting for it to be over. Basically, I was flowing and said a few things about Kia that I never thought she would hear. I never once said her name. But I referenced some of the things that happened when we were younger, then I spoke of how sexy she was, how I was waiting for the day that we could be together, and it even got a little sexual. I sighed. I knew I wouldn't be able to deny that the song was about her.

She looked up at me strangely when it was over. I shied away from her gaze as we heard the door bein' unlocked. Ray's grandmother, Miss Pat, walked in, saving me at least for now.

Later Kia and I went to a get-together with Ray-Ray and met up with the old crew.

"Damn, did anyone leave Brooklyn?" Kia asked me with a smile.

I laughed. Everyone was shocked as hell at her new look. All, and I mean *all*, the guys wanted to talk to her. It made me want to stick by her like glue, but I couldn't, she wasn't mine. It was hard watching her flirt with all of the guys. I think she was aware of my feelings, though, because as much as she flirted, she didn't seem serious about any of them. And most importantly she didn't leave with anyone.

Ray-Ray brought his stash and we burned until early morning.

We were high as hell when we got back to my mother's place. We couldn't stop giggling. I unlocked the backdoor and put a finger to my lips.

"Shh," I told her with a big-ass grin on my face. We forgot about the bags by the door and tripped over them. I helped Kia up while we tried to hold in our laughs. I searched for the light switch but couldn't remember where it was. The light clicked on and my mother stood in the entryway. She crossed her arms and we avoided her glare as we tried to stop ourselves from laughing.

"You guys are something else," she said, noticing our bloodshot eyes. She shook her head. "And you think I don't how y'all used to smoke as teenagers either." We both giggled. "How *is* Raymond?" I smiled.

"He's good," I said and she smiled back slightly.

"Yeah, I bet he is." She looked at the clock. "It is four o'clock in the morning. Try to keep the noise to a minimum, OK?"

"We will," Kia told her.

"Goodnight," Mom said as she walked upstairs.

"Night," we called back.

I smiled at Kia as we walked through the kitchen and up to my room. We both lay down on my bed in the dark, quiet for a few moments.

"That was fun," Kia commented after a while.

"Yeah. You were quite popular." I knew she was grinning in the darkness.

"I don't do it on purpose."

"Yeah, right. You were flirting right back."

"If I didn't know any better, I would think that you were jealous."

"Hmph. I think you do know better now." She giggled a little.

"So that song *was* about me."

I decided to admit it. There was no way I could hide it and it was about time I told the truth to her and to myself. Plus, I was high, and that made me more open anyway. I propped myself on my elbow and looked into her face.

"Obviously."

"Why didn't you say anything sooner? How come I had to find out like this?"

"I didn't know how to say it. Besides, you were dating a lot, as usual, and when Terrance came along I didn't think I had a chance."

"But we talk about everything." I shrugged.

"I thought my actions were pretty clear. I mean, you can read me better than anyone."

"You still should've said something."

"How do you feel about it now that you know?"

"It explains a lot." I chuckled.

"That's it? Goddamn." I lay back. "I should've known. See why I didn't say anything?"

"Well, it's a lot to process. We have a history together and it's not something to be entered into lightly." I leaned on my elbow again.

"Sometimes it's best not to think. Sometimes you should just do." I kissed her lips softly then and she responded, placing her hand on my cheek and kissing back. She pushed me away when it got intense.

"Wow," she said. She stood up. "We, umm, we're both high and this is something that umm . . . we shouldn't do it, not this way," she stammered. I sighed as she walked to my bedroom door.

"I'll see you in the morning," she told me.

"Yeah," I said as I lay back again.

She walked out and I didn't know what to think. She was holding back just like I thought she would.

Kia

". . . it's a lot to process," I told David. He was finally honest about his feelings and that was the best response I could think of. I didn't know if I was ready to give in completely, not after what had happened the last time I was ready to be honest with someone about my feelings.

He shocked the hell out of me when he kissed me. I'd be lyin' if I said that I didn't like it, but I had to push him away. We were both under the influence and as much as I wanted him, I had to think rationally. I wanted to remember every stroke, every lick, every thrust, and I couldn't do that high. I stood up.

I tried to explain, but the words, they just didn't come out right. I was flustered and bent. He exhaled as I walked over to the door. I knew he was pissed, but one of us had to be thinking sensibly.

"I'll see you in the morning," I said sadly.

"Yeah," he replied as he lay back on the bed and looked at the ceiling.

I felt so bad.

I tried to apologize to him the next morning, but I don't know if I got through to him.

"Don't worry about it," he told me.

"But you're mad at me now."

He looked into my eyes as we sat on the couch.

"I'm not mad, Chunky."

"Are you sure?" He nodded and stood up. "I'm 'bout to go to the barbershop and get a shapeup. You can come with me if you want." I shook my head solemnly. He smiled and touched my chin.

"Don't look like that, please? I told you, I'm fine." He shrugged. "I kinda expected this." I nodded in understanding. "I'll see you when I get back."

"OK," I replied.

My cell phone rang as he walked out the front door. I clicked it on.

"Hello?"

"Hey, where are you?" I heard Karen say on the other end.

"Brooklyn," I told her.

"Damn, you just left without sayin' nothin' to nobody?"

"Well, I figured you were still mad at me."

"That's not the point. You should've lemme know so that I didn't walk into an empty condo." I laughed.

"Sorry. Next time I'll letchu know whether you're pissed at me or not." She laughed too. "Are you still mad, though?" I asked.

"No, not really. I'm sorry about that. I was just hurting and I needed someone to lash out at."

"It's alright. I'm used to being your scapegoat." She laughed again.

"I'm not that bad, am I?"

"Sometimes you are."

"So, what are you doing in Brooklyn anyway?"

"Me and David are visiting his mother."

"I know it's cold as hell over there, huh." I laughed.

"Yeah, but it was hot last night."

"What do you mean by that?" she asked curiously. "You met some new guy up there?"

"Not exactly."

"What, you and David actually hooked up?" she asked with a giggle.

"Actually, yeah. I mean, kinda. He kissed me last night."

"Ohhh," she cooed. "Just a kiss, though?"

I smiled and proceeded to explain the entire situation to her from the song, to bein' high, to the way I had to leave his room.

"Wow," she said when I was done.

"I know," I said, fake sobbing. "And now I don't know what to do. I wanted him so bad last night, but it just wasn't the right time, feel me?"

"Yeah, you shouldn't do that while you're not in your right mind."

"I know, and that's why I stopped. But now I think I totally messed up any chance I had to be with him."

"Is he pissed atchu?"

"No, he said he wasn't, but he's gotta be hurt by it."

"Aww, that is a real shame."

"I know. What should I do now?"

"Just wait it out. If it's meant to be, it'll just happen, right?"

CHAPTER 7

Kia

Over the next couple of months or so, David and I just didn't talk about what happened in New York. I did what I always did when I wanted to avoid a subject. I threw myself into work. Plus, Candice had started takin' yoga and Pilates classes to get back in shape after the baby was born, so I went with her. I even started a stricter diet. My body was tight. By the end of the second month I was looking better than I ever had, and I liked it.

David seemed to make himself even scarcer after that, though.

I walked into my kitchen one night while he was out. I was havin' a serious craving, so I decided to cheat on my diet a little and opened up my freezer. Way in the back, where I would *not* be able to see it under normal circumstances, was a pint of Chunky Monkey ice cream put there for emergencies like these.

I opened up the carton, took off the plastic, and tried to stick my spoon in. It was a little hard so I put it in the microwave for like twenty seconds. When the microwave beeped, I grabbed the ice cream. I hoisted myself up onto my counter and stuck my spoon in. Then I stuck the spoon in my mouth.

Mmm, I thought, *melted just the way I like it*. Yeah, I needed this.

I heard my front door being unlocked and froze a little. I could hear his footsteps as he walked through the living room to the kitchen. I hid the carton behind me.

"Hey," David said with a smile when he reached the doorway. He looked at the clock on the coffee maker. It read three AM. "What are you still doin' up?" he asked as he dropped his keys on the kitchen table and slipped out of his Tims.

I smiled sheepishly and revealed my pint of ice cream. He laughed.

"You caught me," I said. He read the carton.

"Chunky Monkey, huh? What happened? I thought you were on a health food kick."

I smiled again as I put the spoon in my mouth and took another taste.

"Moment of weakness. Is that horrible?"

He smiled back as he looked into a drawer and grabbed his own spoon.

"No," he said as he took a taste of the ice cream as well. "Mmm. Good."

"I know, right?" He nodded.

"This sight is actually quite comforting," he told me as he sat next to me on the counter.

"How so?" He looked into my eyes.

"Reminds me of the good old days. Chunky Monkey was your favorite ice cream, remember? It's how—"

"I got my nickname," I finished with a grin.

It was true. I used to tear up some Chunky Monkey back in the day. And when I was about six or seven, Momma started calling me "Chunky". Then it just stuck, and pretty soon everyone was calling me that.

"But that wasn't the only reason," I said as I hopped down off the counter. I pulled up the oversized T-shirt I was wearin' to reveal my black boy-shorts and flat stomach, belly button ring and all. "And that chubby little girl is no more. I ain't goin' back to that. I've worked too hard for this body to see all my efforts go to waste."

I looked up into David's eyes. He'd froze with the spoon in his mouth and I recognized that expression. I'd seen it thousands of times in the eyes of many other men. Lust.

Just lookin' at my body had given him a hard-on. I dropped my shirt. Then I smiled coyly and rinsed my spoon off in the sink.

"What, no more ice cream?" he asked.

"Nope."

"Butchu've barely eaten any."

"I'm good. I just needed a taste to kill a craving. I'm 'bout to hit the sack."

He nodded and I started to walk out of the room. I turned back though with another coy smile.

"Good night, David."

"Night," he replied.

"Mmm," I moaned. "Touch me right there."

His body was rock solid, and his skin was the color of dark cocoa, just the way I liked 'em. But he was faceless to me as his hand moved in between my legs and stroked.

"Ooh, yes," I sighed. "Just like that."

He kissed my neck and I was hot. It felt like my insides were on fire. His lips moved to my right breast and sucked. He stuck a finger in me and his other hand massaged my left breast. I moaned again and then I grabbed for his dick. It was so hard and thick.

Just as I was about to put it inside me . . .

I woke up. I looked around my room. The windows were open and my white curtains blew from the breeze that came through them. I turned onto my back and looked at the ceiling.

"Damn," I said to myself. "What was that about?"

I closed my eyes and tried to fall back asleep, but that dream had made me too horny. I put a pillow between my legs to try to suppress the feeling, but that only made the material of my biker shorts rub against my clit, making shit worse.

I put the pillow back beside me and sighed, trying to remember the last time I'd had sex.

Damn, when was the last time I'd had sex? Couldn't have been that long, could it? I realized that I hadn't been on a date in a while either. *What the hell happened to me?* I asked myself. *When did I fall off?* And silently I answered myself. My crush on David had made me forsake the need for male companionship and as a result, I'd let my sex life wane too.

But right now, I am too aroused and I need a release. I looked at the clock—four o'clock. Who could I call? At the moment I couldn't think of anyone worth calling, and my address book was downstairs. And as far as David went, well that in itself was a delicate situation, so I took off my shorts and started touching myself. I sighed as I used my other hand to massage one of my breasts and tweak the nipple. It felt good, but I wanted more. I turned my lamp on the lowest setting and opened up my nightstand drawer. I searched for my rabbit. I hadn't used it in a while. There was no need to; there'd always been a guy around to satisfy me. So it was *way* in the back of my drawer when I found it.

I took off my shirt and lay down, taking the cover off my pink and white vibrator. I turned it on. It hummed and the top rotated. I put it against my clit first, teasing myself. I massaged my breast again and sucked in air. Then I put it in my mouth, just to get it wet enough, and put it inside me. I let out a low moan as I moved it in and out. *Yeah, this is what I needed*, I thought. I was so excited that it brought me to the brink in a matter of minutes, and then I gasped, in surprise.

I heard my bedroom door creek open and I looked up for just long enough to see a head duck out. I turned off my vibrator, although there was no mistaking what I'd been doing. There was no way I could cover up that sound.

"David?" I called as I pulled my sheets closer to my chest.

He walked fully inside my room. He had on just a pair of blue boxers and I could see each ripple of his abs in the dim light. He had a guilty expression on his face. I guess he thought that I would be mad, but when he saw that I wasn't, his face changed. No words were spoken as he walked over to the side of my bed.

He pulled my covers back and surveyed my curvy frame for a moment as I looked up at him. And that was the second time just looking at my body made him hard. He knelt down and I licked my lips as he took the rabbit from me. He turned it back on and eased it inside me slowly.

"Mmm," I moaned as he looked into my eyes.

He licked up my chest and kissed my neck. He pecked my lips then he moved to my thighs, kissing and licking them all over as he caressed them.

"Oh, David," I said as he started to move the vibrator in and out of me faster.

He stopped abruptly, making my pussy throb. It yearned for more. He put the rabbit in my mouth and watched me suck on it. Then he placed it on my nightstand. He moved to kiss me tenderly, deeply. His tongue stroked mine and he sucked on my bottom lip gently. The kiss gave me butterflies. It also made me wonder how good he would be at giving head.

As it turned out, I didn't have to wonder for long.

When his head moved between my thighs, he did not disappoint. He stuck his tongue inside me first and then moved it ever so gently around my clit. He'd found my weakness. There was nothing that drove me crazier than getting eaten out, the right way. And nothing was more erotic than looking down and seeing a man's head between my legs. Nothing made me cum harder. I bit my bottom lip to stop me from screaming, but he made a move that made me lose all composure. He sucked in my clit and then flicked his tongue across it—once, twice, three times. An orgasm rumbled through my body.

"Oh shit . . . Oh my god . . . Oh yes," I cried and then I had to grab a pillow to cover my face. I started whimpering as I bit down on the pillow. It felt so good.

He gave me a moment to recover when he was done and then he stood up. His boxers dropped to floor and I knew that it was my turn.

He started to get on top of me, but I stopped him when I stood. I kissed his lips and then I pushed him to sit down on the bed as I got down on my knees, ready to suck that big, beautiful, black dick.

David

Kia smiled at me as she walked out of the kitchen.

"Goodnight, David," she said.

"Night," I replied and then I put the cold carton of ice cream against my hard-on.

That woman was somethin' else and I wanted her so badly. I'd tried to suppress my feelings after we left Brooklyn, but every time I looked at her all I could think about was being with her. Pretty soon I just avoided it all together, until tonight that is.

I got down off the counter and put the ice cream back in freezer, not sure about what to do. Kia wasn't someone I could just have sex with and then walk away. Of course I wasn't opposed to the idea of being in a relationship with her. I knew deep down that she wanted more, although she would never admit it. And therein lies the problem. She wouldn't commit even if I was to stay. It was definitely a Catch-22. Either way, I'd lose. But, goddamn, was she ever sexy.

I walked into the living room and sat down on the couch, deciding to watch TV and try to take my mind off everything. I got more comfortable and lounged across the sofa. I dozed off after about fifteen minutes.

When I woke up, I was harder than I was before I fell asleep. It was about quarter to four when I went upstairs to take a long, cool shower. It helped a little.

I put on some boxers and started to walk down the hall toward my room. Then I noticed that Kia's bedroom door was opened a crack and dim light shown through. I walked up toward the doorway and listened, just to see if she was awake.

I could hear her searching through her nightstand for something. She closed the drawer and then I saw her. I could see her reflection in the full length mirror on her closet door. She took off her shirt and was now completely naked. And that's when I noticed what was in her hand, what she'd been searching through her nightstand for—a pink and white vibrator. My jaw dropped and I thought I should leave, but my feet just weren't moving.

She lay back down on her bed and I heard her turn it on. I could hear her breathing get heavy and then I heard her moan. I had to see. I pushed the door open quietly and stuck my head in a little. Her eyes were closed. She was moaning and playing with her nipple. I could tell that she was about to cum soon. If I could just open the door a little bit farther . . . *creek.*

She gasped and looked up at the door. *Shit*, I said to myself, *I'm caught out. She is about to crucify me.*

I heard the vibrator being turned off as I moved to make my way down the hall.

"David?" she called.

Damn, I thought. *Why didn't I just go to my room? Why did I have to be so goddamn curious?*

I shook my head as I walked back and stepped into her room. She pulled the covers up over her chest, but she didn't look mad. Actually, she looked just as horny as I was. She didn't say anything, so I took a chance and walked over to the side of her bed. She still said nothing, so I pulled the covers off her and looked at her naked body. It was surprisingly flawless—not a stretch mark, not a scar, and it looked so soft. Her pussy was groomed perfectly, too—not a hair outta place. Even her toes were immaculately manicured, and she had a silver toe ring on her middle toe. I was as hard as ever now.

I knelt down and she licked her lips as I took the vibrator from her. I turned it back on and looked into her eyes as I slid it back inside her. She was extremely wet and she moaned as I pushed it deeper and deeper. I kissed her breasts and then her neck. I gave her a quick kiss before I moved down to her thick, beautiful thighs. I moved the vibrator faster as I kissed and licked them.

I stopped without warning and pulled it out. Her breathing was staggered as I turned it off and put it in her mouth. I watched her suck it as she looked into my eyes. That shit turned me on. I took it out and placed it on the nightstand. Then I kissed her. I kissed her slowly, sucking off every trace juice from her lips. And I wanted more. I faced her toward me, her legs hanging over the side of the bed, and buried my face in between her legs. She tasted so sweet and I savored every bit of it. It didn't take long for her to cum, and when she did, her body started trembling. And she moaned and screamed and cried out things that were just barely audible. She grabbed onto a pillow and I think she may have even started crying.

I let up and gave her a moment to catch her breath. Then I stood up and took off my boxers, more than ready to be inside her, but she had other plans. She shocked me by standing up and pushing me to sit down on the bed. She kissed my lips before she got down on her knees.

She didn't go straight for my dick. She licked my balls first. Lovingly she sucked each one of them into her mouth.

"Oooh, mmmm," I moaned as her tongue stroked them so good.

She then moved her lips down my dick slowly. Goddamn, they were so warm and wet. I was getting more aroused by the second. She moved up and down, swirling her tongue around the shaft. She almost brought me over the edge a few times, but each time she would slow down, and after a while I noticed that she was doing this on purpose. It was sweet torture. I'd never had someone control my dick like she was doing. By the time she was ready, I'd laid back on the bed and didn't think I could hold it any longer. She had me moaning, and for the first time in my life I had a toe-curling experience, literally. I grunted as I exploded. Sitting up, I watched as she swallowed every ounce—the freak.

She let up and smiled at me. I just shook my head with a smile and lay back down. I couldn't move. My body tingled and I was so relaxed as I looked up at the ceiling.

Kia

I looked up at him with a smile when I was done. He smiled back and lay back down on the bed.

I got up and left the room. I went to use the bathroom and get something to drink.

"David?" I called when I came back. He'd turned off the lamp.

"Hmm?" he answered, already half asleep. I held up my juice as I walked over to the bed.

"You want somethin' to drink, babe?"

He looked into my eyes and I looked down at him as he smiled.

"Naw, I'm good, thank you," he said. He held out his hand. "Come lay with me."

I smiled as I put my glass down on the nightstand and laid down next to him, my head on his chest and his arm around me as I pulled the covers up over us. I figured we weren't gonna have actual sex that night, but hell there was always tomorrow, and he'd satisfied me in more ways than any other man ever had.

I awoke with a smile, but it faded as soon as I realized that I didn't feel David's presence beside me. I sat up and looked around—no note. I grabbed my cell. No missed calls or voice mails. I sat and listened for any indication of someone else in the house, but I didn't hear anything. I wanted to cry, but I told myself, *Don't panic. Maybe it isn't whatchu think. He could've just stepped out or, something.* But my internal words of reassurance did little to comfort me as I got up and went into the bathroom.

Two o'clock now and he still hasn't called or anything. I didn't know what to do with myself. I'd never felt so crazy inside. I'd never had to wait by the phone or anything like that. I had never let myself. I'd always felt that I was too good of a woman to be waitin' on any man. If he couldn't find time to treat me as good or better than I treated him, I was gone. But with David . . . it was different. I don't think I'd ever cared about anyone as much as I cared about him.

Why is it that the guys we like never seem to like us back? Why did they do us so wrong?!

I was so frustrated, but needed to make my way to the studio. Maybe it would take my mind off of him. Oh, the songs I could write about this.

An hour later I was finishing up a short session when David walked into the studio. My heart skipped a beat as I watched him give Tyrone dap. I didn't know what I was gonna say to him, but I knew I had to say somethin'. There was absolutely no way I could let this go. Last night happened and we were both gonna have to own up to our actions.

"OK, Kia," Tyrone said from outside. "Come on out the booth, shorty."

I nodded and put my headphones back on the stand.

I walked out and smiled at David. He smiled back.

"I have to talk to you," I told him. Tyrone eyed both of us. I knew he could sense a different aura between us. "In private," I added as I gestured at the door. David nodded and walked out with me.

"What's up?" he asked when he reached the hall. I shrugged.

"I was just kinda wondering happened to you today?"

"Oh, nothin'," he said nonchalantly. "I went for a run and then I went out with Kareem."

"OK," I said slowly. "You couldn't call nobody?"

"I'm sorry. I just figured that you didn't want me jockin' you or anything." I gave him a confused expression. "I mean, nothing's changed between us, right?" I glared at him. "And that's the way we both want it, right?"

I crossed my arms and shook my head. I couldn't believe what I was hearin'. I couldn't believe it was happening to me again. Just when I thought I was on the same page with a guy, he threw me for a fuckin' loop.

"So what, I was just someone to suck your dick last night? Some chicken-head that you're gonna discard like nothin'?"

"What? No!"

"And there I was waitin' by the phone for ya ass."

"OK wait, I think we got our lines crossed somewhere—"

"No, I think you made yourself quite clear, David."

"Kia—" he started but I was too through.

"Listen," I said, cutting him off, "I'm gonna be at my mother's house until about eight. Have your shit outta my place by then."

"What?"

"Have your shit gone and get gone. I will have the locks changed tomorrow."

"Kia, you can't be serious."

"As a heart attack."

"Wait a minute—"

I put my hand up to stop him. There was a pause as I looked up into his eyes.

"I thought you were different." With that, I walked off.

I broke down and started cryin' when I got to my car. I'd never been so hurt.

My phone rang as I started the car. I looked at the ID. Liyah.

I sniffed and clicked it on.

"Hello?"

"Uh-oh, you sound like you've been cryin'," she said. "What's wrong?"

"Are you at Momma's house?"

"Yeah."

"I'm on my way over now. I will explain everything when I get there."

David

I woke up the next morning and looked over at Kia. I smiled. She looked so peaceful.

I got up slowly so as not to wake her and went into my room to change into shorts and a T-shirt. I went into my bathroom, brushed my teeth, and washed my face. Then I went out for my run. I met up with Kareem at the basketball courts afterward. We gave each other dap.

"Wassup, man?" Kareem said.

"Nothin'," I said nonchalantly. Then I figured that I had to tell him about me and Kia. He *had* liked her and I didn't wanna cause any conflicts. "Actually, that's a lie," I began. "There is something that I need to tell you."

He looked at me curiously as we sat down on the bench beside us.

"OK, what's that?" he asked.

"Well, me and Kia kinda hooked up last night."

He raised his eyebrows, but I couldn't tell if he was mad.

"Hooked up?" I nodded. "Well, there go my dreams of marriage and kids," he said with a sigh as he looked away from me and across the courts.

"Huh?" I was confused. He started laughing.

"I'm only jokin'," he said with a grin. I laughed too.

"Oh, you had me feelin' all bad."

"Don't feel bad about it. Things happen. I had a feelin' you liked her anyway."

"Was I that obvious?"

"Lil' bit," he told me, holding up his index finger and thumb to show me.

"Well, I'm glad you're not pissed at me. I didn't know how to tell you."

"Don't even worry about it, dawg. What happened between me and her wasn't that serious anyway."

"What exactly *did* happen between y'all two?" I asked.

"Oh, umm, nothin'," he said. But they'd been running that same game since that night and I was *not* buyin' it. I looked at him skeptically. "OK, I'll just say that it is waaay too embarrassing to talk about and we can leave it at that." I chuckled.

"Aight, I guess I can live with that."

"So, what's gonna happen with you and her now?" I shrugged.

"I don't know. I think I might leave it alone. You know how she is about relationships."

"Right, but you and her have this history together. It

ain't like a plain old one-night stand."

"You're right, but she ain't the clingy type either, and I don't wanna push a commitment on her, feel me?" He nodded.

"I'm sayin', though, you and Kia fit together. It should've been you two all along." I smiled.

"I know."

I went home after I left Kareem at the court.

"Kia!" I called when I walked inside, but I got no answer. I was disappointed. I'd hoped that I would see her before she left for the studio. I looked at my watch and thought maybe I could still catch the end of her session.

I went upstairs to take a quick shower and change, and then headed out. Kia was finishing up in the studio when I walked in.

"What up, Tyrone?" I said, giving him dap.

"Chillin' as usual, man. You?"

"Same." He pressed a button on the panel.

"OK, Kia," he said, "come on out the booth, shorty."

She put her headphones on the stand and walked out. She smiled at me and I smiled back. "I have to talk to you," she said and I nodded. She glanced at Tyrone behind me. And that's when I remembered that she told me he'd liked her. *I hope this thing me and Kia got goin' on ain't gonna cause any problems between me and him*, I thought. "In private," she added. I nodded again and we both headed out to the hallway.

Then the part that confused me happened. I don't know what I said to piss her off, but she just went kinda crazy on me.

"So what?" Kia said. "I was just someone to suck your dick last night? Some chicken-head that you're gonna discard like nothin'?"

"What?" I said, in shock at the way she was reacting. "No!"

"And there I was waitin' by the phone for ya ass."

Oh, shit, I thought, *What have I done?* "OK, wait," I said, "I think we got our lines crossed somewhere—"

"No, I think you made yourself quite clear, David."

I felt bad. This hadn't been my intention. I thought I was givin' her what she wanted, and I wanted to explain all that if she'd let me.

"Kia—" I started, but she cut me off again and proceeded to tell me that she wanted me out of her house. Now she was just bein' irrational. If only she'd let me explain.

She looked up into my eyes sadly and I felt like a jerk.

"I thought you were different," she said and then she walked off.

I am *different*, I wanted to say, but Tyrone stuck his head out of the studio door. I knew he'd heard the tail-end of the conversation. Actually, he'd prob'ly heard more than that.

"Everything OK out here?" he asked with a kinda smirk.

I glared at him. He didn't know shit about what had just happened, and I wasn't about to explain myself to *him*. He'd prob'ly been rootin' for us to fail all along.

Kia's vocals blared from the studio. It was the song she'd been workin' on when I walked in.

"*How could you have me waitin' by the phone? How can you be so cold?*" she sung and I knew she was talkin' about me.

Tyrone smiled and it took everything I had in me *not* to punch him in the jaw.

I walked down the hall with a shake of my head.

I did head to Kia's and gather my things that night. Two weeks later I hopped a plane back to New York after a few too many unreturned messages, some hang-ups, and dismissed advances.

PART THREE:

CAN WE MAKE THIS RIGHT?

CHAPTER 8

Kia

"So who's gonna be at this party?" I asked Karen. She was now my assistant, and I was getting my hair and makeup done.

A year had passed and I'd released my first album a few months ago, so I had to be any and everywhere to promote it and get my name out there. That night we were in Manhattan. David was also promoting an album. It had already gone double platinum, so there was a huge possibility that he'd be at any big industry parties, especially the ones in New York. And I wanted to steer clear of that at all costs. So far I'd done a pretty good job of it.

"Not sure," she said as she looked through a clothing rack trying to help me find somethin' to wear.

"Not sure?" I glared at her. "You know you're s'posed to check." She frowned at me.

"Don't scold me, aight? You know that after we left ATL there wasn't time for me to do much of anything. I don't think you can avoid him anymore anyways. Both of you are about to blow up. Besides, it's been a year. You should be over what he did to you."

I sighed, knowing that she was right.

"I don't know how to get over it." She looked at me seriously.

"Well, I hear he's engaged now."

"Oh, that makes me feel a whole lot better. Thanks," I replied sarcastically. She put her hand on my shoulder.

"I just meant that you should use that to get over your bitterness toward him. He's moved on and so should you."

"She's right, you know," Candice added. She was now my personal hair stylist and makeup artist. "You're bein' all mad while he's obviously not even thinking about you. It's just a waste of energy, hun." I sighed again.

"I know, I know." There was a pause. "But I wrote a great album because of it," I said with a smile. 'Ren smiled.

"True dat, girl," she said. Candice had finished my hair and Karen came over and put her arms around me. We looked at each other in the mirror. "You're too beautiful to be pining away for some guy. They should be falling at *your* feet."

I smiled again and she kissed my cheek.

"Come on. We need pick out somethin' hott for you to wear."

"Somethin' to make him regret ever dissing you," Candice agreed. "That way if he is at this party, you'll get the last laugh." I nodded.

"I don't know what I would do without you guys, seriously. I think I would be in a mental institution or somethin' if it wasn't for y'all," I joked.

"You're welcome, sweetie," Karen said with a laugh. "Now let's get you into the dressing room."

We picked out some cute jean culottes with a black "I Love New York" T-shirt that we cut into a halter-top as a joke. We also cut a jean jacket into a shrug. I wore black heels and a black fedora over my newly razor cut and layered hair. My jewelry was diamond chandelier earrings, silver bangles, and a cute silver anklet. My makeup was flawless, thanks to Candice, and I was ready to turn heads. Bein' bitter had definitely thrown some salt into my game, and it was time that I got back out there.

Turned out that David *was* at this party with his fiancée. She was cute, I guess—light-skinned, skinny, tall with short hair—a definite contrast to me. I'd wondered if he'd done that on purpose. He wore a dress shirt and jeans.

His hair was cut short, and there were two huge diamonds in his ears. He'd finally grown a mustache on that baby face of his, too. I noticed him starin' at me a couple of times, actually, more than a couple, but I pretty much ignored him the entire night.

Kareem caught up to me at the bar.

"Hey," I said brightly as I hugged him. "How are you?" I asked when I pulled away.

"Good," he said with a smile. "You?"

"I been alright. Workin' a lot."

"Yeah, I've noticed. Your new video is hott." I smiled.

"Oh, thanks."

"You *and* Dave are doin' big things now, huh," he said, cutting off the small talk and getting straight to the point with a sincere look in his eyes. I was suspicious.

"Did he send you over here to talk to me? 'Cuz it's not gonna work," I told Kareem. He held up his hands in innocence.

"No, this ain't a scheme. I promise." I sighed.

"How is he?" I asked.

"He misses you more than he lets on."

"Yeah, he missed me so much that he asked someone else to marry him," I said with an attitude.

"What was he s'posed to do? Sit and wait for you to come to your senses?"

"Excuse me, but I didn't leave him hangin'. It was the other way around."

"It wasn't like that," Kareem started, but I spotted Karen gesturing to me from across the room.

"I'm sorry, but I have to go," I told him. "It was good seein' you."

I didn't let him respond, just walked away.

That chat had left me upset. It prob'ly had a lot to do with why I left with a guy that night. I walked right past David, too, without as much as a care.

"Hey, Momma," I said as I walked through her backdoor.

She smiled and kissed me on the cheek.

"When did you get back?" she asked.

"This mornin'," I told her as I sat down at the kitchen table. "It was crazy in Manhattan, Ma."

"Really?" she said as she walked away from the fridge. She was cooking as usual. "Did you go to a lot of parties?"

"Did I ever." She looked into my eyes with a smile.

"Did you see David at any of these parties?"

I smiled back. My mother didn't know anything about what had happened between me and David. I'd sworn Liyah to secrecy. I liked it this way. I'd get an update on him every time I walked through the door. I was mad, but I liked to know that at least he was alive.

"Yes," I said. "He was at this one party with his fiancée."

"His what?" my mother asked in shock as she turned fully to face me.

"He's getting married, Momma. I thought you knew." She shook her head. "Wow, this is a first. I found out somethin' about him that you don't already know."

"Pam didn't mention it when I talked to her last."

"Maybe she doesn't know yet," I said with a shrug. "I just found out my-damn-self."

"What does she look like?" my mother asked curiously. I crinkled my nose.

"She's OK. Tall, gangly, high-yellow with short hair." She laughed at my description.

"Sounds like you're jealous."

"Neva that, Ma," I lied. "She ain't nothin' compared to this." I stood up in my jeans and T-shirt, holdin' out my hands with a smile. She laughed again.

"Here's somethin' I betchu didn't know. Pam is finally moving to California."

I sat back down. Now *I* was in shock.

"Really?" I asked.

"Yeah. David bought her a house here. And it is gorgeous, too, from what I hear." She'd turned around again so she didn't notice my mortified expression. "In a couple of weeks I'm gonna have a barbecue. . . ."

I'd tuned her out by then. If Miss Pam was moving out here, that meant that I'd see a lot more of David than I bargained for 'cuz he'd be visiting every chance he got. And I didn't know if I was ready for that.

David

"Chrissy!" I called as I walked through the door of my penthouse.

I lived in Manhattan now. So much had changed in just a year. My album was doin' well on the charts. And I had a new woman—Christina Jackson, an around-the-way writer from Massachusetts. Tall, light-skinned, thin—she was pretty much the exact opposite of Kia, in personality too. She was reserved and quiet, didn't like to party, and was a generally good woman. I never admitted it, but I was still mad about the way things had ended between me and Kia, especially because I never got to tell my side of the story.

But I did love Christina. And I figured it was about time for me to settle down. That was why I asked her to marry me.

"Chrissy?!" I called again as I walked through our living room and up the hall.

She was in the den at the computer as usual, prob'ly typin' another novel or poem. And she had headphones on, music blaring.

I walked over to her and slid my arms around her gently. She looked back at me with a smile and I kissed her lips as she pulled off her headphones.

"You and that headset," I said with a smile. "I been callin' you since I got through the door."

"Oh, I'm sorry, baby," she said. "I was just so into this story I'm writin', and you know music helps me zone out." I shook my head with another smile as I walked toward our bedroom.

"Anybody call while I was out?" I asked.

She followed me into the bedroom and stood in the doorway as I got undressed.

"Kareem called and said somethin' about a party tonight. Be ready at ten." I nodded and looked at her as I stood there in just my boxers.

"That shit is gon' be live, boo. You should really come with me."

"No, I'm cool with stayin' home. You know how I feel about those things." I grabbed her hands and pulled her into me.

"Baby, please?" I pleaded. "You never come with me. I need you to run interference, tell all those women to back up off me," I said a grin. She punched me in the arm playfully.

"You betta be runnin' interference yourself," she told me. I backed her up until she lay on the bed with me on top of her.

"Please?" I asked again. "Puh-leese?" I pouted. I planted kisses on her neck. "Please. Please. Please." She laughed.

"That tickles, Dave." I tickled her sides in response and she went crazy. "OK! OK! OK! I'll go!" I stood up.

"Victorious!" I yelled as I raised my arms in the air.

"Yeah, yeah, yeah," she said, pulling me back down and kissing my lips. "Don't let it go to your head, though. And it is just this once, aight?"

"OK," I answered. I pulled her up. "Join me in the shower, woman."

She giggled as she followed me.

That party was hott. And I was havin' a good time until Kia walked in.

I don't know if I was bein' naive or what, but the fact that she might've been at this party hadn't crossed my mind. The minute I saw her, it turned my entire world upside down. She wore jeans, a hat, and a black "I Love New York" top, probably as a message to me. She looked beautiful. Seemed like she got more beautiful every time I saw her. It forced me to face the fact that I still had feelin's for her. And it took all of my will power not to go up and talk to her.

Kareem walked up to me through the crowd after we'd been at the party for a couple of hours.

"Can I talk to you right quick?" he asked close to my ear so I could hear him over the music. I nodded and then looked at Christina, who was sittin' at the table next to me. I bent down and kissed her on the cheek.

"I'll be right back, OK?" I said quietly into her ear.

She smiled up at me and nodded. I kissed her lips and then walked a few feet away from her with my boy.

"So have you noticed?" he asked as he gestured at Kia. She was dancing and giggling, the life of the party as always. I nodded crossly.

"How can you not notice her, man?" He looked at me in genuine concern.

"You OK to stay a little longer, or do you wanna leave?"

Before I could answer, Kia walked right past us with some Hispanic guy. She left the party with him. I shook my head in disbelief as Kareem raised his eyebrows at me.

"I'm ready to go, dawg." He nodded in understanding and gave me dap.

"I'll see you at the studio on Monday."

"OK," I replied as I walked back over to Chrissy. "Hey baby, you ready to go?" I asked. She looked worriedly at me.

"Yeah, I guess. You OK?" I smiled slightly.

"Yeah, just tired."

She stood up and kissed my lips.

"Let's go home."

That night I made love to Chrissy, but I thought of Kia. I went down on her and every time she screamed my name, I imagined it was Kia.

"Hi, sweetie," my mother said to me a few weeks later

as I walked through the doors of her new house in Cali. I'd bought it for her recently as a surprise. I wanted a way to repay her for everything that she'd done for me as a child. I'd known that she'd always wanted to move closer to Kia's mom, so when I got the money, I moved her out her to LA. "What do you think?" she asked as she gestured at the living room. She had just gotten brown leather couches, an entertainment center, and beige curtains. I smiled at her.

"Nicely done, Mom," I responded. She grinned up at me as I pulled her in for a hug. "Are you happy?" I asked her simply. She thought for a sec.

"I think I'm the happiest I've been in a very long time," she said. I smiled at her again and kissed her cheek. Chrissy walked into the room from the kitchen just then.

"Aww," she said with a smile when she saw us. We both smiled back at her. "This house is massive," she stated. "For just your mom, I mean."

"Well," I said as I pulled her into my arms as well, "it's not just for her."

She looked up at me curiously as my mother beamed at my side.

"What do you mean?" she asked.

"I mean, this isn't just her house. It's our house." I looked down at her. "If you want it, that is." I knew she wanted it. She had always said that moving away from the east coast was one of her dreams, and I wanted to give that to her.

"What?!" she exclaimed in disbelief. She wildly kissed my cheeks. I laughed.

"I'll take that as a yes," I said, and then hugged both of them.

I walked up to the house with blue shutters with mixed feelings. So many memories. I'm sure Kia had thought about buying her mother a new house, but I knew Miss Anita would not have it, this place was her home. The backdoor was ajar as usual when I walked onto the back porch. I knocked on the door.

"Miss Anita!" I called. "Anybody here?!"

"Just me," Liyah said as she walked up from the basement. "Momma stepped out."

"Hey," I said with a smile. She smiled back as we hugged. "How are you?"

"Good," she replied as she crossed her arms. She gestured at the window where we could see my car. "That your Benz outside?" I nodded, grinning. "Doin' big things now, huh? Come a long way from that little boy I used to beat up." I chuckled as we both heard someone barreling up the porch steps.

"Hey, Liyah, whose . . ." I heard Kia's voice say as I turned around. "Benz," she finished when she saw me. I couldn't help but think of how beautiful she was in just jeans and a white T-shirt. Her hair was pulled up into a ponytail, none of it in her face, and she had on no makeup. We stared at each other for a moment and for the first time in my life, I couldn't read her expression as she looked back at me. She broke the gaze first and looked past me at her sister. "Momma home?" she asked and Liyah shook her head. "Tell her I stopped by, OK?" Liyah nodded and Kia glanced at me one last time before she headed back out.

I panicked. I was desperate to talk to her.

"You have to go after her," I told Liyah as I faced her again. "Get her to talk to me."

"Why, Dave?" Liyah asked. "From what I hear, you did her dirty."

"Liyah, what happened, it's not whatchu think, I promise. I could explain that to her if you'd stop her."

We heard Kia's car speed off. I sighed.

"You tellin' me the truth?" Liyah asked. I nodded.

"It was all a huge misunderstanding, I swear. But she never lemme clear it up. If I could just talk to her, Liyah . . ."

She was nodding as she picked up the cordless phone and dialed.

"Kia," she said after a moment or two, "come back over here and talk to this boy. . . . Chunky, he says it was all a big misunderstanding. . . . I don't know. You'd have to ask him that. . . . I know, sweetie, but he seems sincere to me. . . . Please? Do it for me, OK? . . . Alright. . . . OK, bye." She hung up and looked at me. "You owe me big."

I smiled as I went up to her and gave her a huge bear hug.

"How 'bout a house?" She giggled.

"I'll settle for a Beemer."

"Candy-apple red?"

"You know it."

I chuckled and gave her a huge kiss on the cheek. We heard Kia's car outside again a second later. And then she slowly walked up the porch steps and back into the kitchen.

"Good luck," Liyah said to me. She squeezed Kia's arm on her way out the backdoor.

Kia crossed her arms from her spot across the kitchen and I noticed that her face was flushed. I hoped she hadn't started crying because of me. There was an uncomfortable pause. "So, say whatchu gotta say," she finally told me.

Kia

I drove over to my mother's house and noticed the silver Benz before I even pulled up into the driveway. Liyah's car was at the far end near the garage, Momma's car was no-where to be found.

I ran up the steps of the back porch, curious to see who the visitor was, but when I got inside he turned around and looked at me. I was a jumble of emotions as we looked into each other's eyes. I didn't know whether to yell at him, cry, or jump into his arms. I'd missed him and I hated him all at the same time. I was the first to break eye contact when I looked at my sister. I asked if Momma was home, even though I knew that she wasn't. When Liyah shook her head, I took one last quick look at David before I headed back out.

I ran to my car when I stepped off the back porch, hopped inside, and sped off. But I didn't go far. I just drove down the street and parked on the side of the road. I needed to regain composure before I started to cry. I sat back in my seat and closed my eyes, breathing deeply to try to stop the tears. Only one fell as my cell phone rang. It was Momma's ringer—"Mercy, Mercy Me" by Marvin Gaye.

I wiped my tear away as I picked up the phone, knowing that it was only Liyah.

"What," I said as I clicked on.

"Kia, come back over here and talk to this boy," she said.

"Talk to him about what? About how he dissed me? How he left me high and dry that day?" I asked angrily, and then tears actually did start to fall.

"Chunky," she started, "he says it was all a big misunderstanding."

"And what the fuck is that s'posed to mean?"

"I don't know. You'd have to ask him that," my sister told me calmly.

"He hurt me so badly, Liyah."

"I know, sweetie, but he seems sincere to me."

"I don't know if I can talk to him. I don't know if I'm that strong."

"Please?" Liyah pleaded. "Do it for me, OK?" I thought for a moment and then wiped my cheeks again.

"Alright, I'll talk to him for you, but I make no promises of resolving anything."

"Alright."

"I'm up the street, but gimme a moment to get myself together. I don't want him to know that I was crying over him."

"OK, bye."

I clicked off and grabbed some tissues out of my glove box. I wiped my face and then blew my nose. I pulled down my visor mirror and looked at myself. My face was a little red and my eyelashes were wet and sticking together. I searched my purse for any kind of makeup, but found none. I grabbed another tissue and wiped my eyes again.

"This is gonna have to do," I told myself as I put the visor back up.

I put the car in drive and proceeded to turn around.

I parked back in the driveway and walked back up the steps. I leaned on the doorframe when I walked inside. Liyah wished him luck and then squeezed my arm before she walked outside. He looked at me with concern in his chocolate-brown eyes.

Shit, I thought, *he can tell that I was crying*. I crossed my arms and there was a pause.

"So," I said, "say whatchu gotta say." He gestured at the kitchen table.

"Have a seat with me?" he requested. I hesitated. "Please?" I didn't say anything, just pulled out a chair across from him and sat down.

"First of all," he began, "I want to apologize for leaving you like I did that morning. I had no idea it would cause so much trouble, and maybe if I hadn't left, things would be different between us."

He stopped like he was waiting for a response from me, so I said, "Go on."

"Kia, I never, ever meant to hurt you. You gotta know that."

"Butchu did and I don't understand why. Everything was so perfect that night and then it just . . . I've never had my heart broken so bad."

"You're right. Everything *was* perfect. You satisfied me in so many ways."

"Then what happened? Why didn't you want to be with me?"

"I did. I wanted to be with you, but I didn't think you wanted the same thing."

"What?"

"You were Miss I-Don't-Need-A-Man. Plus, after what happened in New York, I didn't think you wanted to be with me."

I looked at him in surprise. This was news to me.

"Oh," I said simply. "Well then, why didn't you just tell me this?" He smiled slightly.

"Because you never gave me the chance. You never returned my calls or anything. You even hung up on me a couple times. I got tired of tryin'."

I'm an idiot, I thought. *This is all because of* my *hard-headed ass.* I looked down at my hands first and then back into his eyes.

"I'm sorry, David. God, I am a jerk," I said with a small smile. He chuckled.

"I'll forgive you on one condition."

"What's that?" I asked curiously.

He didn't say anything. He just grabbed my hand and pulled me toward him for a warm hug. I hugged him back tightly. He smelled exactly the same—Axe deodorant and Curve cologne. Feeling his arms around me after so long made me emotional. A tear fell from my eye.

"You'll never know how much I missed you, Chunky." I smiled.

"I missed you, too." He looked into my eyes.

"You cryin'?" he asked with a smile as he wiped my cheek. That made me cry more as I laughed.

"Just so many emotions inside and after so long, I . . . I'm sorry for everything." I looked up at him seriously. "None of this would've happened if it wasn't for me, and I'm so sorry."

He wiped my cheeks and kissed my forehead, pulling me into his arms again.

"Don't worry about it. I'm just glad that we could clear this up." I noticed the clock on the microwave as I pulled away.

"Oh shit," I said. "I gotta go." David looked into my eyes.

"I'm leavin' in a week," he said. "When will I see you again?"

I thought. My mother's cookout was three days away, but I knew that wasn't what he meant.

"You busy tomorrow?" I asked. He shook his head. "Meet me at the park at four then. You know the one." He smiled and nodded. "And bring some skates witchu."

He nodded again and I headed out the door. Liyah was sitting on the front porch when I walked over to my car.

She walked up to me.

"Everything OK?" she asked in concern. She could see that I'd been crying again.

"Yes," I said with a smile. "Everything's perfect. They were happy tears." I shrugged. "Turns out this whole thing was my fault."

"Really?" she asked in surprise. I nodded.

"I'm sure he'll explain it to you. We're meeting each other tomorrow." She raised her eyebrows.

"Wait, Kia. I wanted you guys to make up, not rekindle a romance. He's engaged, hun."

"I know," I told her seriously. "I won't put myself in harm's way. I promise." She looked at me skeptically. "Don't worry, OK? I know exactly what I'm getting myself into."

CHAPTER 9

Kia

"Kia!" my little cousin Tasha called. I had just walked into the park.

Her braids swung as she ran over to me and I hugged her. She'd grown a few inches since the last time I'd seen her, and she had some curves on her thin frame.

"Wassup, girl?" I said. "How you been?"

"Good."

"How's your mom? I haven't seen her in a while."

"She's good. Actually, we'll be at your mother's barbecue." I nodded and then she gestured at her friends, some of the girls from one of the dance classes I used to teach. They were playin' double-dutch beside us. "Wanna play?"

"Oh no. I haven't jumped in so long."

"Come on," she pleaded. "Like when we were younger, please?" I smiled and put down my skates.

"OK, but only a couple of jumps. I'm here to meet someone." She nodded and we walked over.

"Can my cousin get a couple of turns?" Tasha asked. The girls nodded.

"What do you want play?" one of them asked. I thought for a moment.

"How 'bout 'Hey Concentration'."

They all nodded and started turning. I jumped in. They sang as I jumped.

"Hey, hey, hey, hey concentration, where have you been? Around the corner and . . ." It was fun, and I actually wasn't as rusty as I thought I would be.

"Hey," Tasha said when I finished, "remember our competition number?" I laughed.

"Yeah, you?"

She nodded and turned to her friends. She explained to them how to turn. They started turnin' slow. I jumped in first. Tasha jumped in, facing me.

"Faster," I said to the turners. We played numbers, criss-crossed our legs, then I held her foot and she back-flipped. "Faster," I said. We hopped. "Little faster." We moved to turn and hop, and my feet got caught in the rope. "Aww," I said with a laugh and Tasha giggled with me. I noticed David watching from a few yards away and gestured for him to come over.

"Hey," I said with a grin.

David

"I'm gonna miss you," Chrissy said as we hugged. We were at the airport and she was catching a flight back home. I kissed her lips.

"I know, baby," I said with a smile. "But I have to stay for this barbecue or I would never hear the end of it, trust me. I'll be home in a few days, I promise." I grinned. "Then we can start makin' some moves to head back out here for good." She smiled back.

"I can't wait. I'm so excited." She looked at her watch. "I wish you could stay with me until the plane gets here."

"I know. Me too," I said, feelin' a little guilty as I lied. I was s'posed to meet Kia at the park in about a half hour, but I couldn't tell Chrissy that. "Kareem wants me at the studio ASAP. He wants to remix a couple tracks." She pouted.

"OK," she said slowly. "I'll see you when you get home." I nodded and put my arms around her again.

"Call me when you get there." She nodded back and we kissed one last time.

I headed back to my car, feelin' a little low. I'd never been the liar or the cheatin' type with any of my other girlfriends, but there was a desire in me that could only be fulfilled by Kia, and that was the only thing I could think about as I drove to the park.

I spotted her as soon as I walked in. She was playin' double-dutch. It took me a matter of seconds to find her. She always stood out in a crowd. She had on daisy-dukes and a black halter top since it was so hot out.

I smiled. This sight took me back. We used to come to this very park when we were younger. It was where all the kids hung out during the summer. And even then, I could spot Kia in the same spot with her girls playin' double-dutch or sitting on a bench gossiping with them. I had such a huge crush on her then. I'm surprised she never noticed. I used watch her jump rope as I shot hoops from the basketball court. And every now and then we'd catch each other's eye. Then she'd smile. That pretty smile. If she knew how weak she made me when she smiled, she could've controlled my every whim.

Back then, I wanted to be with her, but I was too afraid of what people would think and say. I chuckled to myself thinkin' about how stupid it was now. It seemed like light years behind us when I thought how far our relationship had come.

Kia missed a step and the rope collapsed. She started laughin' with the young-girl she was jumpin' with.

She noticed me watchin' and gestured for me to come over.

"Hey," she said with that same bright smile. I smiled back. She looked at the girl next to her. "You remember David, right?" The young-girl looked at me.

"Uh-uh," she said with a giggle after a few seconds.

Kia laughed too, figuring I wouldn't remember her either. Kia introduced us.

"David, this is my little cousin, Tasha. Tasha, David." We nodded at each other. "Anyway, I'll see you lata, OK?" Tasha nodded and they hugged. Kia waved to the other girls. "See y'all."

"Bye," they said in unison, but that was before they

really noticed me. I waved at them and they immediately started gigglin' as they waved back. I think they were too nervous to actually come up to me though because none of them did.

"Oooh check you out, 'Big Time'," Kia teased, but I just chuckled as we walked off.

On any other day I would've walked over and at least hugged the girls, but today wasn't about that. Today, I was spending time with my number one girl. I gazed down at Kia for a moment, happy to spend at least one evening with her before I had to leave her again.

"What," she said with a shy smile as she tucked her hair behind her ear. I smiled back and shook my head.

"Nothin'."

She picked up her rollerblades and then noticed my empty hands.

"You didn't bring any skates witchu?" I shook my head.

"I figured that I would just rent some when we got to the boardwalk." She nodded and then she looked up at me.

"So tell me something," she said as I looked back at her curiously, "where did you tell wifey you were goin' today?" I looked away from her.

"The studio. She left, on her way back to Manhattan." She studied my expression after I said that.

"You look like it kills you inside to lie to her." I shrugged.

"It does. This is way outta character for me."

"Well, David," she said, "nothing has to happen that you don't want to happen. You know that, right?"

I nodded, but thought, *That's the problem. I want it all to happen.* But I didn't say anything as two teenage girls walked up to her. One was curvy and chocolate-skinned like Kia. The other was a little more heavyset with caramel-colored skin.

"Excuse me," the curvy one said, "aren't you Kia Haughton?" Kia nodded.

"Yes, I am." They both held out notepads.

"Can we have your autograph?" the heavyset one asked. Kia smiled.

"Sure." She took the pen she was offered and signed for both of them. "Y'all got the album yet?" They both nodded.

"We both like that one song you got on there called 'Curves,'" the curvy one said.

"Oh, thank you," Kia cooed.

"Is it true?" the other asked.

"Is what true, sweetie?"

"Is it true that you were chubby when you were younger?"

"Oh, yeah, girl," Kia answered with a wave and a sort of laugh. "My nickname was 'Chunky' back in the day. They still call me that." The girls laughed.

"You let them call you that?" the heavyset one asked. Kia nodded.

"Yeah."

"I'da punched all of 'em."

Kia giggled, but said, "It never bothered me, you know why?" The girls shook their heads. "'Cuz my momma always told me that I was beautiful. She never made me feel any less than anyone 'cuz I was heavy, and that gave me the confidence and strength to hold my head up high every single day no matter what anybody said about me."

"So why'd you lose the weight then?" the girl asked.

"I got tired of bein' outta breath every time I walked up a flight of stairs," Kia joked. The girls laughed again. "And," she said on a more serious note, "I had some health issues." She started to list them as she counted on her fingers. "Asthma, high blood pressure, I was even on the verge of diabetes. So . . ." She held up her hands and showed off her figure.

"You're really strong," the curvy one said.

"I'm a woman, baby girl," Kia said with a smile. "We all have it in us. It just takes a little bit of work to find it. Remember that." The girls nodded. "What school do you guys go to?"

"Belmont High."

"Oh, for real? That's my old high school."

"We know," they said in unison as they both grinned. Kia laughed.

"Betcha didn't know that I'll be doin' a benefit concert there in a month or so."

"Really?" the heavyset one asked.

Kia nodded and put her arms around both of them.

"Tell you what, I wanna chill wit' y'all that entire day. You guys can come back stage and everything. How's that sound?"

The girls slapped hands in excitement. Kia got their information and then they were on their way.

"Sorry 'bout that," she said to me as we started walking again. I smiled.

"Don't worry about it." I looked into her eyes. "I didn't know you had all those health problems." She shrugged. "That was really cool, whatchu did for them, I mean." She shrugged again.

"Those kinds of girls are the reason I wanted to do what I do. They need a voice, ya know?" I smiled.

"I have a confession to make."

"What's that?" she asked curiously.

"I had a crush on you when we were teenagers, but I was afraid to admit it." She laughed.

"You know, Momma said that she thought you did, but I told her she was crazy. It was the weight thing, right? That's why you didn't admit it?" I nodded guiltily.

"I was a shallow motherfucker." Kia laughed again.

"It's OK, I understand. Sometimes it's hard to get over your hang-ups."

"It probably would've happened eventually anyway. Sometimes I feel like me and you were together in another life or somethin'."

We reached the skate stand and I grabbed a pair of size twelves. We sat down and changed into our rollerblades. I stood up and realized that I had to get used to the feelin' of being on skates again. It'd been years since me and her did this. Kia got up with ease, though. It was like ridin' a bike for her. She'd always been the better skater. All those years of dance class had made her madd graceful. She danced around me in the skates with a smile.

"What's wrong?" she asked. I had yet to move. I laughed.

"I'm so afraid that I'm gonna bust my ass any second now." She giggled.

"Aww. Come on. Take my hands." I held her hands and she pulled me along, skating backwards. She did that until I got comfortable and was able to let go, actually skating on my own without falling. But I did grab her hand as we skated up the boardwalk.

"I forgot how much fun this was," I said.

"Me too. I forgot how much fun all of it was, like playin' double-dutch. I hadn't jumped since freshman year." There was a pause as a cool breeze moved through the air. She looked up at the sky. Clouds were covering the setting sun. "It's s'posed to rain tonight."

"For real?" She nodded. "I hope it doesn't start 'til later, 'cuz I don't want this to end."

She smiled at me, but said nothing as we rolled farther along the boardwalk. There was a reggae band playing up the way. Kia tugged on my hand so that we could stop and listen. We both bobbed our heads. She couldn't resist and went up to them, dancing in her skates.

I smiled and couldn't help thinking, *Chrissy would never do that*. The two women were complete opposites. That was the way I'd wanted it. But now that fact made me even more torn. I loved different qualities in both of them.

The band smiled at Kia as the song changed. Kia smiled back when she realized that they were playing one of *her* songs with a reggae beat. She raised her eyebrows at me.

"Uh-oh," she said as she rocked her hips to the beat. I smiled at her.

"Sing," one of the guys said.

"Oh no," she said, embarrassed.

"Please," he pleaded.

The other guys joined in and she giggled.

"Go ahead, baby," one of them, a dred, told her in his Jamaican accent.

She gave in and started singing the words. Her impromptu concert drew a crowd. Then when they realized who she was, it drew even more people over. And when some kid in baggy jeans noticed *me*, it was all over. It was a little chaotic and we were sitting ducks without our security. If hadn't started raining, we'd have been there all night signing autographs.

We quickly rolled to the skate stand and returned my rollerblades. We changed back into our sneakers as we stood under the overhang. I looked at her.

"I had a really good time tonight," I told her. She smiled.

"Me too. Sorry about all the chaos."

"No biggie. They really love you out here." She nodded.

"I get a lot of support from LA, but I'm sure it's the same for you when you're in Brooklyn." I nodded and then there was a pause as I looked into her brown eyes.

"So what now?" I asked, hoping that she could sense that I didn't wanna leave her. She smiled coyly.

"You tell me," she said as she crossed her arms.

"I don't have anything to do, so . . ." She giggled.

"I'm only messin' witchu, boy. You should know that you don't have to beat around the bush with me. Follow me in you car."

We both made a run for it and then drove to Kia's condo. I looked around as we walked inside. Not much had changed in the past year. That fact was kinda comforting.

"Take off your shoes," she said. I did so. "Come on. Let's go getchu some dry clothes."

"Oh what," I said as we made our way up the stairs, "you just keep men's clothing layin' around."

"No," she replied when we walked into her room. She clicked on the lamp walked into her walk-in closet. "Just yours," she said as she put a small box on the bed.

"What's this?" I asked as I picked up a familiar pair of jeans. She crossed her arms.

"There were some things in the hamper when you left." I looked at her suspiciously.

"Are they clean?" She laughed.

"Yes, fool. You think I would leave dirty clothes in my closet for a year?" I shrugged and laughed.

"I don't know. You were pretty pissed." I picked up a shirt as I said that and pieces of torn photos fell onto the floor. I could see half of my face on one of the pieces.

Kia cringed as I looked back at her with raised eyebrows.

"Yeah, those are just some of the many pictures that I fucked up after you went home."

"Do you have any pictures of me left?" I asked, only half joking.

"Yes, and I still have negatives," she told me, visibly feeling bad. "Like you said, I was pissed."

I nodded, but didn't make a comment on what she said, and that's when I noticed the bed.

"This isn't the same bed, is it?" I asked. The huge oak headboard and footboard had been replaced by a cherry wood, sleigh bed. She shook her head.

"I couldn't sleep in the other one after everything that had happened."

"Lemme ask you a question," I said, lookin' at her seriously. "If I hadn't wanted to talk to you the other day, would you have ever wanted to make up?" She shrugged.

"I honestly don't know." I looked away from her. "What do you want me to say, David? I was heartbroken and I had to deal with it." She gestured at the bed and tattered pictures. "These were my ways. It's not like I went crazy and fucked up your car or somethin'." She smiled. "Although the thought did cross my mind." I smiled back.

"You've got problems, you know that?" She laughed.

"Whatever," she responded as she walked over to her dresser and pulled out a pair of pants and a T-shirt. It thundered loudly just then and she walked over to the window, looking out. "Damn, it is crazy out there." She looked back at me and I again remarked to myself on how beautiful she was. She gestured at her bathroom. "I'm 'bout to take a shower. You can use the other bathroom if you want."

I nodded and watched her walk into the bathroom, closing the door behind her. I gathered my clothes as I heard the water start to run. Then all I could think of was the fact that she was naked in there. I remembered how perfect her body was the first time I saw it. Oh, the curves. She definitely had a body that begged to be touched and licked, and . . . Goddamn. The choice here was an easy one to make. The problem would be dealing with the aftermath.

I placed my clothing back in the box and walked toward the bathroom door. I took my shirt off as I opened the door. I could see her lookin' at me through the shower curtain, but no words were spoken as I peeled off the rest of my clothes and got into the shower with her.

She turned to me with a sexy smile and I took the sponge from her. I slowly ran it all over her body. Then I used my other hand to caress her. Our lips brushed against each others as I leaned over to soap up her ass. I stood upright again and looked into her eyes as she took the sponge from me. She licked her lips. Her tongue moved across my bottom lip as she did it. She soaped me up and then looked back into my eyes. I kissed her passionately then and she kissed me back just as eagerly. We stood under the water and let it wash us. Then I put one of her juicy breasts in my mouth. She moaned as I sucked it.

I turned her around and pushed her up against the wall, and she stroked my dick as her back hit the tile. I was so ready to be inside her, with or without a condom. I trusted her with my life, and I knew that she stayed on birth control. If I was gonna do this, it would be all or nothing. I think she realized that because she looked at me worriedly.

"Maybe we shouldn't do this," she said. I kissed her lips as if to tell her not to worry, and then I slid inside her. I sucked in air.

"Sssssss." Oh man, she felt so good, and the way she

moaned, I knew there was no turnin' back for either of us.

Kia

So there I was, naked, in the shower, with the man of my dreams.

This had been my intention when I got in the shower. I'd hoped he would follow me. I wanted him to, but it had to be his decision. When he did come in, I couldn't tell you how happy I was. But as he pushed me up against the wall and looked at me with so much desire in his eyes, I started to have second thoughts. I looked at him with concern.

"Maybe we shouldn't do this," I said.

His only response was a soft kiss and a look in his eyes, I guess to tell me, "You lured me in here, and we gon' do dis." Then he moved inside me slowly and a low moan escaped my lips. He looked into my eyes and thrust hard the second time.

"Do you want me to stop?" he asked in a low, sexy tone. I couldn't answer 'cuz the way he was grinding his hips into me was driving me crazy. His lips brushed against mine. "Mmm," he moaned. "Tell me you want me to stop." I couldn't. He felt too good. He looked into my eyes. "Tell me you want me." I looked back at him.

"Ooooh, I wantchu, baby," I said.

"Ssss, how bad?" he asked.

"Sooo bad," I told him.

He thrust a few more times and then kissed my lips deeply as he pulled out.

He turned off the water in the shower and then pulled the curtain back. We both stepped out and dried each other off. We walked into my bedroom. David took the box off the bed and then told me to lie down. He smiled at me as I lay down on my back.

"You are so beautiful," he told me as he lay on top of me. I smiled back. "You're perfect," he said and we kissed tenderly. Then he started moving downwards and I held his head as he licked my pussy.

"Mmm, baby," I moaned. "You feel so good."

He didn't stay down there for long. I think he just wanted to make me wetter before he slid back inside. And then he held me close, kissing my neck and shoulders as we made love. It was the most mind-blowing sexual experience I'd ever had. Feeling him cum inside me, and looking into his eyes as he came was the most intimate thing I'd ever done with any man. I wished it didn't have to end.

We lay across from each other, looking into each other's eyes when we were done. He caressed my cheek.

"Are you gonna be here when I wake up?" I asked. I just wanted to prevent myself from going through the same turmoil as last time.

He didn't answer right away. Actually, he looked taken aback at first, and then I could see that he really felt bad about what he'd done the last time. He pulled me closer to him and kissed my lips.

"I'll be here," he said. "I promise." He kissed me again and then we embraced one another. And I slept a little easier knowing that he was the first face I'd see when I opened my eyes.

CHAPTER 10

Kia

I woke up to feel him sliding inside me. He kissed my shoulder and thrust his hips into me from behind.

I moaned.

He moved hard and fast. He moaned as he came, and I gasped. I turned to look at him with a smile. David smiled back and then kissed me.

"That was one helluva wake-up call," I told him with a grin.

"I had to make up for last time."

"You did all that last night."

He smiled again and then looked at the clock across from him.

"It's almost twelve. I have to go soon."

"Oh," I said sadly. "Can'tchu stay a little longer?"

"My mother will be wondering where I am." I kissed his lips.

"Baby, please?" I pleaded with a smile. He thought for a moment.

"OK, I guess I can stay a little bit longer."

"Good, 'cuz I had one last thing that I wanted to do."

"What's that?" he asked curiously.

"Coco Puffs and Saturday morning cartoons," I replied with a grin. He smiled.

"Alright."

I kissed his lips. Then I followed him as he got out of the bed and walked toward my bathroom.

After a bowl of cereal and a few old-school cartoons, he really did have to leave me. I was disappointed, but I knew that we were both livin' a fantasy and it was time for us to wake up.

David kissed me deeply at the door and held onto me tightly. I didn't want him to let go. He looked into my eyes solemnly.

"I guess I'll see you tomorrow." I nodded and looked down at the floor. "Hey, maybe there's a way that we can make this work."

"How?" I asked, looking up at him again. "You gonna break it off with her?" He raised his eyebrows.

"Do you want me to?" I crossed my arms.

"Do you want to?"

He opened his mouth to speak, but his cell phone started ringing.

"It's my mom," he said. He clicked on. "Hello? . . . At Kareem's. Since the weather was so crazy outside, I decided to crash here. . . . I'm sorry. I wasn't aware that I still had to check in with my mother. I'm damn near twenty-five. . . . I know, Mom, but I'm on my way home now. . . Alright. . . . I said alright. . . . Bye."

"Sounds like she was chewin' you out somethin' fierce," I said.

"Yeah, but she'll get over it." He looked into my eyes and then kissed me again. I cut it short.

"Baby, go before you get into more hot water. I've kept you long enough." He smiled and then stroked my cheek.

"Bye." I smiled back.

"Bye."

He walked out the front door, leaving behind the strong scent of Curve cologne on my T-shirt.

David

I drove home, not knowing what the hell I was gonna do about my situation, but at the same time, not regretting it one bit.

I walked through the backdoor and called for my mother. Chrissy came out instead. Now I knew why my mother had been so adamant about me getting home. I looked at her in shock.

"Baby, what're you doin' here?"

"Damn," she said as she crossed her arms and looked at me solemnly. "Don't look so happy to see me."

"It's not that," I said. "I just didn't expect to see you again until I went back to New York. What happened?"

"My flight was cancelled. There was some huge blizzard, which shut down the east coast." She looked down at the floor. "I tried to call you to come pick me up, but you didn't pick up your cell and you weren't here. I had to take a cab back here and I could barely even remember the address. If it weren't for your mom, I would probably still be stranded. Then I finally get here and you were nowhere to be found. I waited up for you all night and most of the day." I felt so guilty.

"I'm so sorry, baby. I was in the studio and I left my phone in the car—" She put her hand up to stop me.

"Don't," she said. "I know you weren't at Kareem's last night, OK? You probably weren't even at the damn studio like you told me either." She looked into my eyes with tears in hers. "I can smell her perfume all over you, David." I opened my mouth, but she put her hand up again. "I never thought I'd be having this conversation with you, at least not this soon. Apparently my mother was right. All men are cheaters, it's just a matter of when."

I sighed and looked down at the floor.

"I can't believe you," she said. "We have got some serious talkin' to do when we get back home, believe that."

With that said, she walked upstairs.

The day of the barbecue was tension-filled. Christina wasn't talking to me, and my mother was mad because I'd made Chrissy mad. And when we got to Miss Anita's, Kia was visibly pissed at me because Chrissy was on my arm. She avoided us like the plague until some family member got to talkin' about how me and her grew up together and pointed her out in the crowd. If I'd had a gun, I think I would've killed myself right then and there.

"That's *the* Chunky? Kia Haughton? Isn't she a singer?" Chrissy asked, the first words she'd spoken to me all day. I nodded. "She's beautiful and far from the chubby little girl y'all keep talkin' about." She looked up at me. "Well, aren'tchu going to introduce me?" I smiled to mask my frustration.

"Sure, baby," I said. I grabbed her hand and led her over to where Kia was standing. She was talking to one of her aunts. Her back was turned, so she didn't have a warning or even time to run away. I called her name. She excused herself and turned around with a forced smile.

"Kia Haughton," I said, "this is my fiancée, Christina Jackson." Chrissy smiled.

"So this is the famous Chunky I keep hearin' so much about."

"That's me, in the flesh," Kia said. Me and her exchanged glances, but I don't think Chrissy noticed.

"It is so nice to finally meet you," she said, moving to hug Kia. Kia obliged reluctantly.

"Nice to meet you too." Chrissy looked at her a little strangely when they pulled away from each other.

"That perfume," she said, "it's nice." She smiled. "What's the name of it?"

Kia smiled back, although I could see in her eyes that she was mortified.

"Actually, it's a mix of different things really." Chrissy raised her eyebrows.

"So it's unique for you, then?"

"Uh-huh," Kia said. "Could you excuse me for one moment, please?"

"Sure," Chrissy said. Kia hurried off and I looked at Chrissy.

"I'll be right back," I said. She nodded and didn't stop me as I walked off.

I followed Kia into the house and into her old bedroom. Purses and other belongings were being kept there. She grabbed hers.

"You'd better get back out there," she said. "She knows you were with me."

"What do you mean?"

"That perfume comment? Dead giveaway. Your cologne was all over me when you left, so I know you smelled like me too." I didn't say anything, but I didn't leave either. "Jesus, she had to have been waiting up for you the entire night." She put her face in her hands.

"Are you OK?" I asked. She shrugged.

"I just feel like the biggest home-wrecking-hootchie-bitch on the planet." She looked up into my eyes. "I thought you said that she'd left." I shrugged.

"I thought she did, but apparently there was some snowstorm in New York and her flight was cancelled."

"Jesus Christ," she said again. "We didn't even use protection," she hissed. Then we heard someone coming up to the door. It was Liyah. She walked in and shook her head at both of us.

"Whatever is going on between the two of you, cut it out, *now*," she told us sternly. She looked up at me. "Your *wife-to-be* is looking for you." I nodded and she walked out. Kia walked out of the bedroom.

"Where are you going?" I asked as I followed her.

"Home," she said when we got to the living room. "I have to go. I can't stay here as long as she's here."

"Wait," I said, "didn't we kind of leave things unfinished yesterday?"

"What do you mean?"

"You asked me if I would leave her."

"And?"

"And, the answer is yes, if you want me to."

She thought for what seemed like an eternity.

"Do you love her?"

"Yes, but, baby, I love you more."

"I love you, too," she said sadly. "But, David, you

made a commitment to her." She shrugged. "Maybe you should honor that."

"What are you saying, Kia?" She sighed.

"I'm saying it was wrong of me to come between y'all. If it wasn't for me, you guys would be happy. If you chose me and you still had feelings for her, things would always remain unfinished between you guys, and then I'd always be wond'rin' what you were doing when you weren't with me."

"But—" She put a hand up.

"Lemme finish. I love you more than I've ever loved anyone, but I messed up my chance. We had our night, baby. Let's just leave it at that." I felt like I wanted to cry.

"Why are you doing this?" I asked. "Why are you pushing me away?"

"'Cuz, she deserves the same chance I had. She deserves a chance not to blow it, like I did." She started to walk out the front door.

"Kia, wait," I said, grabbing her hand.

She turned back, but stopped when she noticed someone behind me. For some reason I just knew it was Chrissy. Kia looked into my eyes.

"I'll see you," she said. And then she pulled her hand away, walking out of my life. I took a deep breath and wiped my eyes. Then I turned to look at my future wife, that is, if she would still have me.

"So," Chrissy started crossly, "she's the one, huh?" All I could do was nod. "When she was pointed out, I recognized her," she went on, "but not in the way that you think. I know she's a singer and all, but I recognized her as the girl that you just couldn't seem to take your eyes off of at that party a few weeks ago." I looked at her in surprise. "Didn't think I noticed?" She waited for an answer, but I didn't really have one, so she went on. "After I saw her here and then found out that *she* was that little girl in all those pictures I'd seen, I was a little confused. Why hadn't you introduced me? What the hell was goin' on? Then I smelled her perfume, and it all started to make sense." I finally spoke.

"I don't really know what you want me to say. I'm

sorry about everything. I'm sorry about the way you found out. I can understand how embarrassing it must be." She shook her head.

"You don't know the half of it, David, trust me." She thought for a moment. "You know what I want you to say? I want you to say that that one night meant nothing to you. I want you to truthfully say that she means nothing to you. That would make it easier on me, and maybe we could fix whatever has gone wrong with us." I looked into her eyes and really wished that I could say I felt nothing for Kia, but it would've been a lie, and I'd done too much of that already. Tears welled up in her eyes. "You can't say it, can you?"

My mother and Miss Anita walked in laughing then, abruptly stopping our discussion for the moment. Chrissy tried to hide her tears, but she didn't do a very good job.

"Christina," my mother said, "are you OK, sweetie?"

Chrissy wiped her cheeks and cleared her throat, but it didn't help. She started to cry harder. My mother went over to hug her as she glared at me.

"Come on," she said. "I'll take you home." She looked at me. "Car keys?"

I started to hand them over, but Miss Anita beat me to it.

"Take mine. I parked across the street, so you won't have any interference." My mother took the keys and shook her head at me in disapproval as they walked out. Miss Anita crossed her arms. "Trouble in paradise?" she asked.

I hung my head dejectedly and then it was my turn to walk away.

Kia

" . . . We had our night, baby. Let's just leave it at that," I told David.

He looked at me in such a way that it hurt me deep inside.

"Why are you doing this?" he asked. "Why are you pushing me away?"

How was I gonna explain this to him? I asked myself. How could I say that I simply just felt for the woman because her heart was being broken, just like mine had been. I told him that she deserved the same chance I had, and then I started to walk out. I didn't wanna cry.

"Kia, wait," David said as he grabbed my hand.

As I turned back, I wanted to take everything I'd said back and just jump in his arms and kiss his lips. But Christina walked in, and I knew I'd made the right decision. I looked into his chocolate-brown eyes for I what I thought would be the last time for a long time, and told him goodbye. I pulled my hand away from his grasp and walked out the front door.

Liyah was waiting for me when I walked over to my car.

"I can't believe you—" she started, but I interrupted.

"Please don't start with me. You don't know what I just did in there."

"Well, Kia, we need to talk about whatchu did in general, 'cuz that shit wasn't right."

"I know, Liyah. But I love him."

"So does she."

"You don't think I know that, god." I sighed. "I thought she was on her way back to Manhattan. Had I known she was even gonna be here, I would've left it alone, trust me. She's gonna have him for the rest of her life. I just wanted one night. As selfish as it was, I just wanted to be with him even if it *was* only for one night." I wiped a lone tear that streamed down my cheek. "Now, we can close this chapter of our lives and move on." She raised her eyebrows at me.

"So, you gave him up for *her*? Why?" I shrugged.

"'Cuz it was the right thing to do."

Liyah hugged me then. I guess she felt bad for tryna tell me off.

"Where are you about to go now?" she asked. I shrugged again.

"Home. There's nowhere else I really feel like goin'."

"You want company?" I nodded. She took my car keys from me. "You're in no state to drive right now." I nodded again and got into the passenger side of my car.

Crash!

Liyah and I screamed as we jumped from our seats on the couch. We were at my place in the living room the next day, and we'd just heard what sounded like glass breaking from outside. We got up to look out the window.

"Kia!" We saw Christina standing next to my Acura with a bat in her hand. "Get your home-wreckin' ass out here!!"

"Oh shit," I said as I noticed that one of my back windows was broken. "I'm going to kill this crazy bitch." I headed for the door, but Liyah stopped me. "What are you doing?" We jumped again as we heard another crash.

"Think rationally, Kia. You can't just storm out there."

"What?! She just broke two of my car windows. What the hell am I s'posed to do?!"

"OK, it's just a car. You have the money to fix it. But what if you go out there and she comes after *you* with that bat? Or what if she's got some other weapon hidden?" I thought about that and nodded. "I'm sure the security on the property has heard all the commotion. I'll call the cops. You call David."

She grabbed the house phone as I grabbed my cell and we heard another crash—my front passenger window.

"Kia!!" Christina shouted. "I know you're in there!!"

I dialed David's number. He picked up after three rings.

"David?" I said. "Jesus, I hope you're close by."

"Actually, I'm right down the street from you, headed to my mother's house. Why, Kia, what's goin' on?" he asked. I screamed as we heard another crash. "What the hell was that?!" he yelled.

"You have to get over here," I told him. "Your girl has gone crazy. She is over here fuckin' up my car!"

"What?!"

"You need to get over here and calm her down before

she does somethin' worse!"

I screamed again. She'd just broken my windshield.

"OK, OK, just sit tight, I'll be there as soon as I can."

"Please hurry!"

We both hung up and I looked out the window again. Liyah was still on the phone with the police.

"Kia?!" Christina called me again. "If you don't get out here in three seconds, I will throw this bat through your living room window!!" I looked at Liyah wide-eyed.

"What the hell am I s'posed to do now?!"

"Go, but be cautious."

I nodded and walked over to my front door. I opened it slowly. She was holding the bat over her head, ready to throw it as neighbors watched from their doors and patios. Some of them were on the phone, probably with the police like Liyah.

"Wait!" I shouted. "I'm here!" She looked at me and then lowered the bat.

She pointed it at me as she came toward me. I didn't know what to do.

"You've got a lotta damn nerve comin' in between me and *my* man."

I put my hands up and tears started to come from my eyes as she put the bat up to my throat and backed me up against the brick wall.

"What the fuck is it aboutchu that's got him so sprung, huh? Why are you so fuckin' special?" she asked.

"I don't know," I answered, not knowing what to say.

"What? You couldn't stand to see him happy with someone else? You had to intervene?"

"No, I just . . ."

"You just what? Come on, spit it out."

"I just love him," I admitted, but that answer seemed to piss her off even more. Rage burned in her eyes.

"Gimme one good reason why I shouldn't beat your ass with this bat right now."

I opened my mouth to speak just as the cops arrived. *Oh, thank God,* I thought. And then I saw David pulling up as well. He hopped out of his car, leaving the driver's side door open.

"Chrissy!"

She turned to look at him and then walked toward him with bat in hand.

"Whoa," he said. "Baby, put the bat down, aight?"

She looked around at the cops and did so. David inched his way toward her. She glared at him and then smacked the hell out of his cheek. He looked shocked, but not mad as she slapped him again, and again as she started crying.

"I hate you!" she shouted as she pounded on his chest. She kept repeating it and beating him and he took it all. Then he wrapped his arms around her and kissed her forehead as she cried.

"I'm sorry," he said. "I'm so sorry."

Liyah came out next to me then. She must've seen how hurt I was watching this entire scene. She tried to touch my arm, but I just shrugged it off and walked back inside my condo.

David

I drove Christina home and we walked into the kitchen in silence. Then we walked to our bedroom with no words. I closed the door behind us. I knew my mother was in the house somewhere.

I just looked at her as she sat on the bed and put her head in her hands. I wanted to shout at her. What the hell had she been thinking fuckin' up Kia's car like that? How did she even know where to find her? But all I said was, "You know she might press charges, right?"

"I don't give a fuck what she does, David," Chrissy replied. "She deserved every single thing that happened. No, actually she deserved worse."

"Just outta curiosity," I said as I sat down on the bed next to her, "what would you have done to Kia if me and the cops hadn't gotten there when we did?"

"Don't know. When I first got there, I just wanted to

scare her. I wanted revenge for everything I was feeling in-side. But when she came out and she said she *loved you* . . . there was so much fury inside me. I don't know. It probably would've been bad."

I raised my eyebrows. I didn't know how to respond. I'd never seen Chrissy really angry before this. I don't think I'd even heard her yell. I never would've guessed that she was the vengeful type, and I must admit that it scared me a little. Guess it's true what they say: it's the quiet ones thatchu gotta to watch out for. One thing was for sure, I'd never cheat on her again. Next time she might come after *me* with a bat or worse. My cheek *still* hurt from the way she smacked me.

"David?" she called quietly, interrupting me from my thoughts.

"Yes, baby?"

She looked up into my eyes as a tear rolled down her cheek.

"Do you love her too?" I thought carefully about my answer to this question.

"I don't wanna lie to you," I said.

"Do you still love me?" she asked after a second of processing my response. I wiped her cheeks.

"Of course." She looked away from me.

"How is that possible?" I shrugged.

"I wish I knew."

"Who do you love more?" she asked, but she stopped me before I could answer. "Never mind. I don't think I wanna know." She looked at me again. "How do we get past this?"

"Good question. I wish I could give you an answer. I wish it was that simple. I wish so many things." There was a pause. "So, you still want me then?" She laughed a little.

"Yeah, crazy as it sounds." She turned to face me ful-ly. "But there will be conditions."

"Like?"

"You have to promise me that you can get over these feelings thatchu have for her and focus on us, our future."

"I promise, baby."

"And we definitely ain't movin' out to California anymore."

I nodded. I'd already expected that.

"OK, next?"

"I'm never leaving you alone at any industry party or function again."

"OK, cool," I said. I'd wanted her to do that a long time ago. "Go on."

"And when you come out to visit your mother, I am by your side every single day while you are out here." I nodded.

"Alright. What about the wedding?" She thought.

"Can we push up the date?"

I furrowed my brow. That was the last thing I'd expected to come out of her mouth.

"Why?" I asked.

"It would just make me more comfortable with everything if we were married sooner. I don't know. My feeling is that a bigger commitment might deter you even more from cheating."

"I guess that wouldn't be a problem if you're sure that's really whatchu want." She nodded.

"It is."

"OK," I said. "We can start making arrangements as soon as possible."

CHAPTER 11

Kia

"Five, six, seven, and! One, two, three, and four . . ." Jaynie shouted.

It was a couple days after the whole car incident and I decided throw myself back into my album promotion a little early. I was rehearsing for tour, and I tried to focus, I really did, but the image of David holding that bitch in his arms kept running through my head. I missed a step and tried to keep going, but I missed another step and Jaynie stopped the music.

"What is going on with you today?" she asked. "I've never seen you mess up like this." I just shook my head.

"Start the music over," I told her. She walked over to the stereo and restarted the track. She counted me in again, and I had to really concentrate on the movement for the first time in my life. Dancing had always been just a natural thing with me, but right now all this emotional bullshit was fuckin' me up.

". . . two, three, triple it up, ball-change, and five, six, seven, shit," Jaynie said as she turned off the track again with a shake of her head. She looked into my eyes. "Do we need to go over the steps again?"

"No."

"Are you sure?"

"Yes," I insisted. "I know the steps. I just got a lot of things goin' on right now and it's fuckin' with me."

"Well, try to forget about it. This is your career on the

line."

"I know, I know." Just as I said that David walked into the studio. I looked up at him. "What're you doing here?" He smiled at me. Jaynie walked over next to me.

"You remember David, right?" I said to her. She smiled up at him.

"Yeah, I remember. He used to come in and interrupt class just like this 'cuz all the girls would be focused on how cute he was." David chuckled and Jaynie looked at me. "Fifteen minute break, 'kay?"

I nodded, she walked out, and I looked up at David again.

"Does wifey know you're here?" He shook his head. "Then maybe you shouldn't be here," I said, kind of with an attitude.

"Hey, *you're* the one that told me to be with her," he retorted. "You know what I want. Say the word and—"

"No, no," I stopped him. "The results of that could be worse than last time, and I'm not dyin' over this shit." He smiled and I smiled back. "What's up?"

He pulled out his wallet and handed me a folded piece of paper. I looked at it. It was a blank check with his signature.

"Oh, David, I can't take this."

"I wantchu to. It's partly my fault that your car is damaged."

"But you know I can easily pay for it. It's not a big deal."

"Yes, it is. Keep it, alright? Whatever the amount of damage, write it in." I smiled.

"How do you know I won't just take advantage? Go on a shopping spree or somethin'?" He shrugged.

"I trust you," he told me seriously.

"Thank you."

"You're welcome." He grabbed my hand and stroked it with his thumb. "I'll be gone in two days."

"Well, it's not like we're never gonna see each other again."

"Trust me, if Christina has her way, we won't see each other for a looong time."

"I hope she realizes that I'm not goin' anywhere. Our families are still tied together."

He nodded and then pulled me into his arms. I hugged him back warmly, trying to hold back the tears.

"I'm gonna miss you," he said.

"Me too, baby," I told him.

He kissed my lips softly and a tear actually did fall from my eye. He wiped it off as he looked into my face.

"Bye," he said.

I couldn't seem to get the word out, so I just nodded and then watched him walk out as the man with the chocolate-brown eyes and the girl with the chocolate skin parted ways again.

David

I straightened my bowtie as I looked in the mirror.

"Here goes nothin'," I said expressionless. Kareem walked up to the doorway in his tux.

"Yo, they waitin' on us, dawg," he said. I nodded and put on my jacket. He walked up to me and patted my shoulder. "You ready?"

"As I'll ever be," I said as I looked him in the eye.

"Hey, don't look so sad, man. It's your wedding day," he told me. "Your bride looks beautiful. So does the church. Everything'll be fine." I smiled.

"Are you sayin' all this to reassure yourself or me?"

He thought for a moment and then smiled back.

"I don't know."

"I don't know either, man," I said, referring to the marriage. "Sometimes, I wonder if I truly did the right thing."

"You sweatin' that *now*?" I shrugged.

"All this shit tends to go through your head when you're about to make a commitment like this."

Kareem didn't comment on what I said as we walked out and up the hall. I don't really think he had an answer for me. I inhaled before we walked up to the altar.

"Just breathe," Kareem whispered to me. I exhaled as we both took our places up there. I looked around the room. I spotted Miss Anita and Liyah in the back of the room. Even Mr. Haughton was there, but no Kia. I didn't know if that was a good or bad thing, but I didn't have much time to think about it because the music started playing.

I felt like my heart was about to jump up outta my chest as I waited for Chrissy to walk up the aisle. And when she did on the arm of her father, I think my heart stopped. She looked so beautiful. I thought, *maybe this* is *the right thing.* That's how I made it through the ceremony.

The reception, on the other hand, threw me for a loop when Kia actually did join us. I noticed her after Chrissy and I had our first dance. She was wearing a gray, pin-striped suit, and her hair was up in a bun. Her eyes were covered by huge shades and she looked like she'd gained a little bit of weight, but to me she was still the most stunning woman in the room. I struggled with that thought as I grabbed a glass of wine and downed it. Kareem came up next to me.

"This is like deja vu or somethin'," he said to me. "What're you gonna do?"

"I'm gonna go talk to her," I said. He raised his eyebrows.

"You think that's a good idea?"

"I don't know, but I have to."

He looked extremely concerned as I walked away, but I didn't care. I hadn't seen or talked to Kia for the last six months, and that desire that I spoke of before was still in me as I walked up to her. She was standing alone looking at the wedding cake. Her back was to me when I gently touched her arm. She turned to me. I noticed that the diamond necklace that I'd given to her a while back was around her neck. I smiled.

"Hi."

"Hi," she said as she smiled back.

"How've you been?"

"OK, I guess. I mean, considering. You?"

"Missing you," I told her honestly.

"I miss you, too," she said quietly. She cleared her throat and looked down at the floor as someone walked past us. I moved to take off her shades, but stopped when I noticed how red her eyes were as she looked up at me sadly. She'd obviously been crying all day. She pushed them back up her nose as another tear fell. She quickly wiped it away.

"Christina looks beautiful. Me, on the other hand—"

"Look more and more gorgeous every time I see you," I interrupted. She smiled again.

"You shouldn't say stuff like that. Someone might overhear," she said. I smiled back. "Listen, I just came to congratulate you. I think I should go before wifey notices I'm here. I'll see you." I nodded just as Chrissy walked up behind her and Kia spoke what I was thinkin'. "Oh. Shit. Look, don't flip out on me, OK? We were just talkin'."

"It's alright," Chrissy said. "I just wanna talk to you." I raised my eyebrows and she looked at me. "David, can you leave us alone, please?" I hesitated. "Please, baby. It's alright. I promise." I nodded and walked back over to where Kareem was still standing.

"Oh no," he said when he noticed the two of them. "Should we go break this up?"

"Naw," I said. "Let's give them a chance to talk."

Kia

"Hi, Momma," I said as I walked into her bedroom the day before David's wedding. "Hey, Miss Pam," I said as I noticed her too. I hugged and kissed both of them. They were trying on matching silk burgundy dresses. "You guys look great," I told them as I sat down on the piano bench by the window.

Momma smiled as they both looked into her full-length mirror.

"Yeah, we still got it," she said. I smiled and silently agreed. They both were curvaceous with small waists, even after having children. Miss Pam started to lay into me as I put my chin in my hands with sadness clearly showing on my face.

"Are you coming to the wedding?" she asked. I shook my head without looking up at her. "Why not?"

"I just don't think I should. There are a lot of things that you guys don't know—"

"You mean there's a lot that you *think* we don't know," my mother interrupted. I raised my eyebrows, looking up at her. "Oh, honey, please. If you and David wanted to hide, you weren't doing a very good job of it."

"It wasn't about hiding it per se, it was just that with the way things happened, we didn't think you guys would think too highly of us if you knew."

"Well, sweetie," Miss Pam said, "we both know that things happen. You can't really help who you fall for, can you? No matter what the circumstances."

"I guess not," I replied as I sat up and rested my back against the wall. "It would just be so hard to see them tomorrow." I looked down again. "Even though I *am* kind of the one who put them that way."

"What do you mean?" Momma asked. They both sat down on her bed.

"I told him to honor his commitment," I told them. They both looked at me wide-eyed and bewildered. "What? Was that not the right thing to do?"

"Well, yeah," Momma said. "We just never knew a woman strong enough to do the so-called right thing."

"Especially when it comes to the man they love," Miss Pam added. "You do love him, right?"

"So much. But our timing was so off."

"Do you think that he feels the same way?" I smiled, thinking about it.

"I know he does."

"Then you just trust that when the timing is right, you two will find your way back to each other."

They both got up to change then, and I thought about that statement. Part of me believed so much that our love would help us find our way back to each other, but the rest of me wasn't so sure.

"I know it'll be hard," Miss Pam went on, "but I still think you should go, at least to the reception. Put on a brave face and make an appearance. Who knows? Despite the circumstances, tomorrow might be the day the timing is just right." I smiled at that thought.

But by the next morning, I was a wreck. I cried right up until it was time for me to go and make that appearance. Since I had gained a little bit of my weight back, I decided there was no way I was wearing a dress. So I put on pin-striped suit over a black corset with high-heeled loafers. Then I put my hair up in a bun, put on some lip gloss, and slid on some black sunglasses to cover my bloodshot eyes.

I turned on the radio as I drove over to hall. Kelly Price's "As We Lay" was playing. "*I know you've gotta hurry home to face your wife . . .*" she sang. I clicked the radio off and drove the rest of the way in silence.

When I got there, I slipped in quietly. The idea was to get in, make sure that David could see that I showed up, and get out. I spotted him with his bride. They were on the floor dancing their first dance, so I decided to wait until he spotted me. Christina's dress was gorgeous—silk, strapless, fitted to the body, and the skirt was all ruffles. Her hair was also pretty—twisted and styled into a perfect bun with beads and flowers framing her face. There was no way I could feel anymore homely. At that moment I wished that I *had* worn a dress.

I turned to look at the wedding cake behind me. It was picture-perfect with five tiers and red roses scattered over chocolate icing. I sighed. I felt so out of place in all of that perfection. And I was seconds away from walking out when I felt a hand lightly brush my arm. I turned to see David smiling at me.

I looked him over with a smile. His tie was a little crooked, he had on his large diamond stud earrings, and his pants were way too baggy. Even in the most formal of settings, David was still David. Leave it to him to make me feel better without even knowing it. And he was still so handsome.

We spoke briefly—telling each other how much we missed one another. Then I congratulated him and tried to slip out before Christina knew I was there. But she walked up behind me before I could leave. *Shit, shit, shit,* I thought when I turned to see her standing there. She told me she wanted to talk to me and after David left, I stood there warily wondering what the hell *we* could possibly talk about.

"May I?" Christina asked as she reached for my shades. I nodded, but looked away as she took them off. She looked taken aback at my red face and eyes. I glared at her as she handed them back to me.

"What did you want to talk to me about?" I asked flatly.

"I just wanted to say that I know whatchu did for me."

I raised my eyebrows, having no idea what she was talkin' about.

"What do you mean?" I asked. She crossed her arms.

"I know that you gave up David for me."

"He told you that?"

"Yes. Actually he more like yelled it at me the other night when we were arguing."

"Oh," I said with a shrug. "Well, I didn't do that for you," I lied, "I did it for David. I only want to see him happy." She glared at me.

"Let's not kid ourselves, OK?" she told me crossly. "You and I both know who he'd be happier with."

"OK. Well, if you know all that then why are you still with him?"

"Because I love him. Nothing changes that. And in spite of your little fling, I know he loves me too. We just got a lot of things we need to work on." There was an uncomfortable pause until she looked into my eyes. "Well, I just wanted to letchu know that I knew, and . . . I wanted to say thank you." She made a face as if the words had put a bitter taste in her mouth. I put my shades back on and crossed my arms.

"You're welcome," I said. "Just, umm, take care of him, alright?"

I touched her arm lightly as I walked out.

PILOT PUBLISHING

PART FOUR:

WILL WE? WON'T WE?

CHAPTER 12

David

I walked out of the studio with another artist. Her name was Shaneel. She was young with caramel skin and shoulder length dark hair. She was doing a hook for one of my new songs. And man could that girl blow. I commented on it as we walked out toward the parking lot.

"Thank you," she said with a smile. "I didn't get to tell you in there, but I am a huge fan of yours." I smiled back. "Never thought I would get to do a song with BK." I chuckled as I stroked my beard.

"You can call me David." She grinned coyly.

"OK then, David." She touched my arm and that's when I noticed Christina walking toward us. She'd grown out her short hair and it was past her shoulders now. She wore a white blouse, pin-striped dress pants with heels, and plenty of jewelry—earrings, madd bracelets, and couple of chains. Most times, all I needed to hear was the jingling of her bangles to know she was home. She stopped a few feet away from us and crossed her arms, tapping her foot impatiently.

I sighed, but looked back at Shaneel.

"Gotta go. See you tomorrow," I said.

She nodded and then walked to her car as I stepped over to my wife. I moved to kiss her, but she shied away from me.

"Who was that?" she asked with an attitude. I furrowed my brow.

"That's the girl I was tellin' you about the other night.

The one who wrote that hook. We started workin' on the song today."

"Hmph," Chrissy grunted. "She's pretty." I rolled my eyes.

"Are you getting at something?"

"She was blatantly flirting with you, David." I groaned.

"No, she wasn't." Chrissy smirked.

"Yes, she was." I shrugged.

"Even if she was, whatchu trippin' for? I'm not interested in her. She can't be more than eighteen. I'm workin' with her. You gon' chew me out every time I work with a female?"

"Only when you work with pretty ones," Chrissy said as she turned around and started walking. I couldn't help but laugh at her response.

"You're out to drive me insane, woman," I said as I followed her to her black Aston Martin. She handed me the keys.

"You drive. I am too tired."

About two and half years had passed. Other than the occasional wave or nod at an industry function, I hadn't spoken to or seen Kia since the wedding. I missed her more than words could say. I got constant updates on her from my mother, though. I knew she'd gotten pregnant and had a little boy.

The first year of my marriage was a rocky one, as one would expect. But the second year had gone smoothly with the exception of recently. Chrissy was just moody as hell for some reason. And she was also madd jealous without cause. I didn't give her *any* reason to suspect anything. I said I wasn't gonna cheat on her again and I meant it. Anyway, no one except Kia herself could fill the void of me missing Kia.

I unlocked the doors and we hopped in. I adjusted the seat and the mirrors. I would be glad when I could get my own car back. It was in the shop for today, just a tune-up. I was so happy it was just for one day. This arrangement would send me to the nuthouse.

"Can I get a kiss now?" I asked Chrissy before I put the key in the ignition. She smiled slightly and leaned over to kiss me tenderly on the lips. I smiled back and drove off. Chrissy closed her eyes and leaned on her hand.

"You OK, baby?" I asked. She smiled and looked at me.

"Yes. I'm just a little sleepy." I raised my eyebrows as we stopped at a traffic light.

"You been exhausted like this for weeks now. Maybe we should take you to a doctor, getchu checked out." She laughed a little.

"I think you're right." She turned a little to face me as I started to drive again. "I have to tell you something."

"What's that?" I asked.

"I'm late," she said.

"Late for what?" my clueless ass asked. She giggled.

"My period, silly." I damn near ran us off the road. "David!" Chrissy shouted as I avoided an accident. I saw an open spot on the side of the road and pulled over.

"Damn, boy," she said when I parked the car.

"Sorry," I said. I turned to look at her with a smile. "Butchu shouldn't tell me that kinda shit while I'm driving." We both laughed. "How late are you?" She smiled again.

"A couple weeks." I thought.

"That *would* explain all the symptoms. Like those damn mood swings." She hit me in my arm with a laugh.

"I haven't been *that* bad." I smirked.

"Yeah, right. I thought your head was gonna start spinnin' a couple-a times." She giggled again. "Seriously, though, we need to go get a test and find out right now." I put the car in drive again.

"My baby might be having a baby," I said with a grin and grabbed her hand as we drove off.

"Two minutes," Chrissy said as she came out of the bathroom back at our place about an hour later. I looked at the clock—eight after six. She'd just taken a pregnancy test. I was a nervous wreck and it showed. She smiled at me and reached up to hug me around my neck. She kissed my lips.

"You alright?" she asked and I nodded. "Come on, we might as well have a seat and wait." She took my hand and led the way into the living room. I sighed as we sat down on one of the couches. "You been quiet since we got here," Chrissy said. "What's goin' on in your head right now?" I lay my head back.

"Lots of things. All the planning and things we have to do before the baby gets here." I smiled. "Is it gonna be a boy or a girl? Which room are we gonna change into a nursery?" She laughed.

"Oh, you had me worried. I didn't know what you were thinkin'."

"Don't be," I said with a smile as I placed my hand on her knee. I looked at the clock again after a moment—six-ten. "Come on, let's go find out the results."

I took her hand this time and led her back to the bathroom. She went in alone and came back out with tears in her eyes. My heart just about broke in a million pieces. She held up the test then and showed it to me, smiling. A plus sign.

"Goddamn, girl," I said with a laugh, "you almost gave me a heart attack." More tears fell from her eyes as she grinned.

"I'm pregnant," she stated.

I grinned and pulled her into my arms, embracing her tightly.

"Yes. And you don't have to worry about anything." I kissed her lips. "I'm gonna take care of you, I promise."

I walked through the front door of my place with Kareem five months later.

"Chrissy!" I called as we walked through the living room. There was no answer. I called her again.

"Maybe she stepped out, dawg," Kareem said. I smiled.

"No, she's probably on that damn computer. She likes to blast music in her headphones while she writes."

He grinned too as we walked into my bedroom. Christina was crouched by the bed holding her stomach. I knelt down next to her as Kareem stood in the entryway.

"What's the matter? You OK?" She looked up at me.

"I don't think so. My stomach's been cramping up all day and it's getting worse. I think something's wrong, Dave." Tears streamed down her cheeks. "What if we lose the baby?"

"Don't think like that." I kissed her forehead and picked her up, cradling her in my arms. "We're gonna getchu to a hospital. You're gonna be fine, and so's the baby." I was saying the words to comfort her *and* me. I was being calm for her on the outside, but on the inside I was really worried. I didn't know what I would do if we lost this baby.

It felt like bats were flying around in my stomach as I waited for the results of Chrissy's tests. I held her hand when the doctor came back. He said that the baby was in distress, and that Chrissy wouldn't be able to bring this baby to full term unless she was on complete bed rest.

So, despite her constant protests, I made sure she stayed in bed. Her mother stayed with us too to help out. We made it all the way to the seventh month without any problems, but then the cramping came back with a vengeance. Chrissy was then put on bed rest in the hospital so that they could monitor her.

But in spite of our best efforts we lost our baby girl in the middle of the eighth month after a still born birth.

Christina really pulled away from me then. It was almost like she blamed me for the loss of our child. I tried to reach out to her, but nothing I did seemed to make her happy.

And after a few months of her distance, I was fed up. I decided to pack my bags and take a break.

I flew out to California to stay with my mother.

Kia

I closed my notebook as I got up to answer the knock on the hotel room door. I was on tour, had been for the last three months or so. And tomorrow I would get a small break because we were ending the U.S. tour in my hometown. I was so excited. I would get to spend a few days with my family, then it would be time to start my six month tour overseas. Yup, almost four years had passed and I was doing big things.

Charles Harris, a short, bald, black man, who was my tour manager, was standing in the hall when I opened the door.

"Wassup, Charlie?" I asked as I let him in. I walked back over to the bed and sat down.

"Well," he started as he sat down across from me, "I have some bad news." I furrowed my brow.

"What's that? And you betta not say someone messed up the schedule." He looked at me helplessly. "You've got to be kidding me," I groaned and then looked into his eyes. "So what happened this time?" He cleared his throat nervously.

"Well," he began again, "things are backed up so much that we, uh, can only spend two days in LA before we have to start touring again."

"What?!" I exclaimed as I stood. "That's crazy. I was promised a week. I haven't seen my family in three months. I won't see them again for six! Who the hell do I have to fire to get shit done right around here?!" Charlie stood up to calm me down.

"Wait a minute. There's no need for all that." I frowned at him.

"Are you kidding me? This is the third time there's been a schedule problem and that was just *this* tour."

"What do you want me to do, Kia?"

"I *want* you to do your job. *You're* s'posed to be overseeing all this shit."

"I'm doing my best."

"Well, your best ain't good enough, is it? 'Cuz this is ridiculous. Now me, 'Ren, and Candice are gonna have problems. And I suppose *I'm* the one that has to tell them, right?" He just stared at me guiltily. I rubbed my temples and sat down. "Just go. You guys are stressin' me out somethin' serious."

He sighed and walked out. I just lay back on the bed, too pissed.

"Hey, Momma," I said when she let me in through the backdoor. She hugged me. It was nine o'clock in the evening and I had just come back from go-sees and a rehearsal for the show tomorrow. I couldn't even say how tired I was.

David's mother was sitting at the kitchen table. I bent down and hugged her too.

"Where is he?" I asked my mother.

"In his room, but he's awake. He's been having trouble sleeping through the night with you gone."

I nodded and walked down the hall to my old bedroom. My son, Jeremiah or J.D., jumped up as soon as I walked in and turned on the lights. He leapt into my arms when I got to his bedside.

"Hi, sweetie," I said as I held him in my arms. "I've missed you sooo much."

"I missed you, too, Mommy," he told me.

My heart was crumbling as I held him. I wanted so much to stay with him longer than just one night. I didn't even want to tell him that I couldn't.

"Sit here beside me. I have to tell you something." I put him down to sit on the bed and he looked up at me curiously. "Remember when I called last week and said that I'd be able to stay with you for a few days before I went back to work?" He nodded. "Well, it turns out that I can't." Tears immediately started to well up in his eyes and I felt like crying with him.

"Why?" He asked as big teardrops rolled down his cheeks.

I wiped them off his medium-toned cheeks and pulled him into my arms again. I kissed his forehead.

"Someone messed up and now I have to leave you early. I'm so sorry, baby."

"But I don't want you to go," he said.

"I don't want to either, but I don't have a choice."

I lay him beside me and looked into his chocolate-brown eyes.

"I'm sorry," I apologized again. "But I promise, this is the last time for a long time." I used my sleeve to wipe his cheek again.

"I heard you haven't been sleeping. Would it help if I stayed with you 'til you fell asleep?" He nodded.

"Can you sing?"

"Sure I can, honey." I went to turn off the light and then lay next to him again, pulling the covers up over us. I started to sing to him and he fell asleep within minutes. Just my presence seemed to soothe him. I wanted to sleep, too, but I was so hungry. I fought with myself for a few moments, but my stomach won the battle as it growled loudly. I kissed J.D.'s cheek and got up, walking back to the kitchen.

"Is he sleeping?" Momma asked. I nodded.

"Did you cook anything? I'm starved." I started to head over to the fridge. She stood.

"Have a seat, baby. I'll get it for you." I smiled as I sat down.

"Thank you."

"You look so exhausted," Miss Pam commented.

"I am," I told her as I rested my chin in my hands. "I feel like just scrappin' the rest of the tour. That's how fed up I am this time. I'm a platinum, Grammy-award-winning artist. I shouldn't have to go through this crap." I sighed. "This is gonna sound funny, but it's starting to feel like work."

"That doesn't sound funny, sweetie," my mother said. "You were happy *and* you were having fun at first."

"I was thinking about pushing the third album back a couple years."

"Oh really?" Momma handed me a hot plate of mac and cheese as she sat down at the table with us. I nodded as I took my first bite.

"I mean, I been gettin' offers to do movies. Even some guest spots on sitcoms and they're all in LA. And even if I had to leave, it would be easier to take J.D. with me on set. I could never do that on tour, at least not now. It's too much. Plus, I can always write songs behind the scenes too."

"Well, that sounds good, hun," Miss Pam said.

"Yeah. It's just hard right now. Every time I leave him, my heart breaks. I feel like I'm abandoning him, and when he cries, I just wanna break down right along with him. I mean, I'm his only parent." Miss Pam glared at me. "You know what I mean," I said with a sigh. "The only one that he knows of."

"Whose fault is that?" she asked. Yes, David is J.D.'s father. I found out a couple of months after I had already told him to be with Christina. I didn't find out I was pregnant until I was already two months along and plans for David's wedding were well underway. And I hid the pregnancy well into my seventh month because I knew I couldn't lie to everyone about who J.D.'s father really was. I figured telling David the truth would do more harm than good, especially where Christina was concerned and Miss Pam resented me because I made her keep it a secret. She only agreed to it because she said I was just as much her daughter as David was her son.

I exhaled again, tired of explaining myself to her.

"He is married now. I'm not gonna have Jeremiah brought up in this crazy love triangle. And I will *not* allow that *crazy woman* to have a hand in raising my son."

"Well, looks like you might not have to," she said. I looked at her curiously.

"What are you talking about?"

"Haven't you noticed the tabloids?" Momma asked. I shook my head.

"I don't read those things. They're mostly rumors."

"And most rumors are based on fact," Miss Pam said. I raised my eyebrows. "Christina and David are still having problems. Paparazzi have been on their tails the entire way. He told me the other day that he's thinking about a separation."

"Really?" She nodded.

"So if those reasons are your only ones for not telling him, then you have your opening now."

I sat back in the chair. I had lost my appetite. I was

too chicken to say anything right now, but it looked like I couldn't run away from the truth anymore.

"Kia?" I heard my name being called. "Kia?" I heard it again as the voice gently woke me from sleep. I opened one eye. 'Ren was standing over me. She smiled. "Wake up, girl. We're home."

I opened both eyes and smiled back.

"Oh my god," I said as I yawned and stretched. "So tired."

I looked out the window on the private plane. I could see LA in its entirety. It was good to be home. I'd just come back from the six month world tour. We'd been everywhere. Actually, we'd just come from China. I was supposed to take a two-month break and then I would talk to my label about possibly pushing back the next album. But, damn, I needed this. We all did.

"I know the feelin'," Karen said. "But you know it doesn't stop, at least not for me." I smiled. She was referring to her husband and two kids. Yeah, Karen had finally settled down. Her husband was a good guy, too.

The pilot announced that he was landing, so we buckled up and waited until the plane was on the ground before getting up and grabbing what we could carry. There was an SUV waiting for us when we got off the plane. They had the rest of our luggage. We got in and they drove to my house first, since it was the closest. I now had a house—nothing horribly extravagant, it's not like a castle or anything, but it did have five bedrooms, three bathrooms, a living room, two kitchens, a den, a game room in the basement, a two-car garage, and a pool. The most luxurious thing in there was a studio, which was built to my personal specifications.

I hugged 'Ren when we got there.

"See you tomorrow," I said.

"Yeah, lata," she said.

The driver helped me bring my luggage in and then they were off. I took a shower, changed into a tank top and jeans, and then I went into the garage.

"Hello, sexy," I said with a grin to my brand new, black, drop-top Lexus. I'd bought it before the tour and hadn't really gotten a chance to drive it. I deactivated the alarm and hopped inside. I smiled. The suede/leather seat was so comfortable. I opened up the garage door, started up the car, backed out of the driveway, and drove off, heading to my mother's house.

I noticed a brand new blue Beemer parked outside Momma's house when I got there that Saturday. I was excited as I parked my car in her driveway.

I grabbed my purse and pulled down my visor mirror. I took out my hair claw and re-clipped my hair up. Then I put on some lip gloss. I hopped out and ran up to the backdoor. It was open, as usual, and I heard his laughter before I even stepped inside. I took a deep breath and walked inside.

He was sitting at the kitchen table with Momma. He wore a T-shirt, jeans, and sneakers. He'd grown a full beard and it was shaped up nicely. They both stood up when they saw me. He smiled at me and I smiled back. Then we moved into each other's arms. We held each other for a long time as my mother looked on with a hopeful grin. I couldn't place the cologne he was wearing, but it smelled really good. I just inhaled and took all of him in.

"It's been too long," David said in my ear.

I pulled away and nodded in agreement. Tears welled up in my eyes. He wiped my cheeks and chuckled.

"You cry every time we do this."

I laughed too and opened up my mouth to speak, but we were interrupted by the ruckus of two little boys clamoring up the basement steps.

"Mommy!" the small one yelled as he ran up to me. I picked him up and kissed his cheek.

"Hi, baby," I said enthusiastically as I looked into his brown eyes. "Miss me?" I asked and he nodded. "I missed you, too, sweetie."

"You're here early," he said.

"I caught an earlier flight so that I could surprise you. I want you to meet someone." I looked back at David. He didn't look shocked, but then why should he?

No one would be if they watched *Entertainment Tonight* or picked up a magazine every once in a blue. And I'm sure his mother told him that I'd been pregnant.

"This is David," I told my son as I gestured in front of me. "He's a very good friend of Mommy's. David, this is my son, Jeremiah."

"Wassup, lil' man?" David said with a smile as he extended a fist.

Jeremiah was wide-eyed and looked at me for approval. He was a little shy.

"It's OK, sweetie," I told him. "Don't be afraid." He took his cue and bumped fists with David. I smiled. "Did you guys get a chance to get your things together?" I inquired of my baby boy. My mother spoke up.

"We were in the middle of it when David showed up." I put Jeremiah down. "Come on," she said as she took his hand. "You too, Bobby," she said to my nephew. She led the two boys upstairs. David looked at me.

"That kid is gonna be a heartbreaker when he gets older."

"Oh, I know," I agreed. "He's already got my mother wrapped around his finger, and he's only three."

"He looks just like you."

"So I hear."

"This is so surreal," he commented.

"What is?"

"Everything. The fact that we're all grown up, havin' kids, and getting married. Where did the time go? I feel like it was just yesterday when we were both two pimple-faced, hormone-driven teenagers."

"Hey, *I've* never had a pimple in my life."

"OK," David said with a chuckle, "that was just me." I giggled.

"Yeah, but so what? You were always gorgeous." David smiled at me and blushed a little. I smiled back coyly. "Still are." I paused as a slight wave of lust rushed through me. "You look so good, David." He licked his lips.

"You do, too," he said with a sexy grin.

Just then my mother and the boys came back into the kitchen so I never got to respond.

"All set?" I asked, seamlessly switching gears. They nodded as I took Jeremiah's bags from Momma. I looked back into David's eyes. "How long you stayin' in Cali this time?" He shrugged.

"Don't know. Might be indefinitely. You know, with all the problems I've been having," he said, correctly assuming that our mothers had already told me the news of his failing marriage.

I nodded and grabbed a pen from my purse. I walked over to the kitchen table and wrote on a napkin.

"Well, here are both my numbers," I said as I handed him the napkin. "Call me, OK?"

He nodded. I grabbed Jeremiah's hand as I walked out.

Karen cracked up laughin' when we were out havin' lunch with Liyah and Candice the next day.

"You really said that?" she asked about my encounter with David.

I nodded with a smile.

"What'd he say?" Candice asked. I grinned then.

"He said I looked good, too."

"Ooh, so what does this mean for y'all two?"

"Not sure yet. He just got back. I told him to call me, though. I hope he does."

"So do we," was Liyah's surprising comment. "It would be about time." I raised an eyebrow.

"I thought you were against me and David's relationship."

"I was never against you guys," she said with a shake of her head. "I was against the fact that he was engaged to be married and y'all were like creepin' around. But now that he's gettin' divorced, I say more power to you."

"Well, honestly, I don't know if he actually is getting divorced. According to his mother, it's only a separation."

"Yeah, but all the tabloids say they've been seen fighting in public and he's been attending events by himself," Candice said.

"OK, but can you really believe those rumors?"

"Probably not," Karen reiterated, "but you *know* they been having problems since before they got married."

"Because of *me*," I told her.

"Well if all it took was one night to rock their entire relationship, then maybe it just wasn't meant to be."

"I guess you have a point," I said.

"Now you finally understand what I went through with Tony," Karen said.

"Yeah, but I was right about Tony."

"Just because he did the right thing doesn't mean that he didn't love me. What's happening with David definitely shows that to be true." I nodded my head.

"I guess you're right." I sighed. "It *would* be nice to be with him again. And it's been so long since I've gotten laid." That was the truth. I couldn't go back to meaningless, and often times mediocre sex after the way David and I had made love. I'd been spoiled. I put my head in my hands as my girls laughed.

"Maybe the wait is finally over," Liyah said. "Maybe this is your chance to finally be together." I looked at them.

"I hope so," I stated. *I really hope so*, I thought.

David

"Dave!" my mother called from the bottom of the stairs.

I popped my head out of my room and looked at her.

"Yes, Mom?" She held up the phone.

"Kareem."

"I'll take it in here," I said with a smile. I picked up and yelled, "Got it," and then put the receiver to my ear. "Kareem, wassup, man?"

"Nothin', dawg," he responded cheerfully. "I been tryna get a hold of you all morning. You don't return messages?" I laughed.

"I'm sorry, but I'm tryna unpack and get settled. You know my damn cell just rings off the hook sometimes. I *had* to turn it off if I was gonna get anything done. How are things in the N-Y?" I sat down on my bed, taking a much-needed break.

"Straight. I'm definitely enjoying this little time off we got."

"Good. How's your better half?"

I could practically hear him grinning through the phone.

"She is wonderful. She's actually right beside me. Hold on a sec." I smiled. Kareem had finally found someone. Her name was Mercedes. She was from Spain and beautiful with her long, dark, wavy hair. And she treated him right. I was happy for my boy.

"David, how are you?" I heard her say in her slight accent.

"I'm straight, considering all the drama I been through."

"That's good to hear. I'm so sorry about you and Christina."

"Thank you, but you know, I'll survive."

"I hope you two can work things out. Anyway, I gotta go finish making dinner for this man. I'll talk to you, sweetie, OK?"

"OK, be safe."

"You too, buh-bye."

Kareem came back on the line a second later.

"So," he began, "have you seen her?"

"Of course I have," I told him, automatically knowing who he was referring to. "You know there's no way to avoid it out here."

"Did you wanna avoid it?" I thought about it and smiled.

"Guess not."

"How did it go?"

"It went alright. She gave me her numbers, told me to

call her."

"Are you gonna do it?"

"Don't know. I mean, I want to, but me and Chrissy aren't really over. It might just stir up more craziness."

"Or it could just help you see who you really want, and if your marriage was in fact a mistake."

"Hmph," I grunted. "You might have a point. But there's another factor with Kia now, too."

"What's that?"

"She has a son now, remember?"

"Oh, yeah. That is somethin' to think about, I guess."

"Yeah, I met the little guy the other day. He looks just like her." I paused. "I'm not opposed to kids, but you know . . ."

"Gotta think about bein' a father figure to someone else's child," he finished. "Gotta think about dealin' with some other man who will never go away. If he's still around, that is. Did she say anything about that?"

"Uh-uh. And I didn't ask."

"The question that you've really gotta ask yourself is do you love her enough to go through more drama? 'Cuz if not, I say just let it go, man." I sighed.

"I don't think I can do that without talkin' to her first."

"Then there's your decision right there. Call her. See what's up. Sort out your feelings. That's what separation is for, isn't it?" I nodded on my end.

"Yeah." But that didn't make the situation any easier.

CHAPTER 13

Kia

"Wow," I said to myself as I drove up to Liyah's new house. It was bigger than mine. At least it looked that way from the outside. We were all growing up, doing bigger and better things. Liyah herself was now married to Robert. Yes, the same Robert that David and I predicted things wouldn't last with a few years ago. They had a little boy, Robert Jr. or Bobby, *and* they were expecting a little girl in two months. How's that for things lasting?

I parked in the driveway and got out to let J.D. out of the backseat. Bobby ran to the car from the backyard.

"Can I go play, Mommy?" J.D. asked, tugging on my shirt.

"Sure, baby," I told him. "Just be careful!" I called as the boys ran around the side of the house. I walked around to the back myself. Liyah was on the deck with her husband, Momma, Daddy, and Miss Pam. Daddy had the grill going.

"Hello, everyone," I said. Hugs and kisses were given all around.

"David's in the house," Liyah said quietly in my ear while we embraced. I smiled when she looked at me.

"Is he now?" She nodded with a grin and hooked her elbow in mine.

"Come on. I need to show you around anyway."

David was coming from the living room when we walked through the kitchen. We smiled at each other. Liyah eyed both of our expressions with a grin. She let go of my arm and said, "I'll leave you two alone."

"I thought you were gonna show me the house," I said.

"This is more important," she told me as she patted my hand. "I'll show you later, or you and David can look around by yourselves."

She glanced back at him and winked before she walked out. We both chuckled.

"Your sister is a trip," David said.

"My sister? She is just as much yours. You can't just disown her when it's convenient." He laughed again.

"Don't I owe you something?" He reached into his pocket and pulled out his wallet. He handed me a hundred-dollar bill.

"What's this for?" I asked, confused. He grinned again.

"You bet me a hundred dollars that Robert and Liyah wouldn't last more than a year. I said six months. That means you win." I giggled.

"Oh, yeah." I slipped the Benjamin in the back pocket of my jeans. David gazed at me then. "What," I said, smiling back as I blushed.

"Come 'ere," he said, holding out his hands.

I put my hands in his and he pulled me into him. He kissed my lips and I kissed him back tenderly.

David

It felt so good to kiss her again.

"I've missed you so much," I told her when I pulled away. She looked up at me with a sexy grin.

"I missed you too."

Her son ran into the room then. We both looked down at him as my mother rushed in behind him.

"I tried to stop him, but he insisted that he come to you," she said to Kia.

She laughed and crouched down to look into Jeremiah's eyes.

"What's wrong, sweetie?" she asked.

"I fell down," he told her, showing her the scrape on his knee. She smiled.

"Well, it can't hurt that bad, hun. You just ran in here without any problems."

"We tried to tell him that," Mom said. "But you know how he can be sometimes."

Kia nodded and stood up. She held out her hand and Jeremiah grasped it.

"I'll put some disinfectant on it anyway." She looked at me and my mother. "Do either of you know where the bathroom is?"

Mom nodded and led the way to the half-bath in the hallway downstairs. I followed behind Kia and Jeremiah. Once we got there Kia picked up her son, sitting him down on the counter. She looked in the medicine cabinet and found Band-Aids along with spray disinfectant. She washed his scrape first and then sprayed it as he cringed from the sting. She put on two Band-Aids and even kissed it. I smiled at the sight until Jeremiah proudly said, "Look, Grandma, they're Blues Clues." He was looking at my mother when he said this.

I furrowed my brow and I looked at Mom in confusion.

"Did he just call you Grandma?"

Mom opened her mouth to speak, but Kia intervened.

"Well, yeah," she said. "She's just as much a grandmother to him as Momma is."

I was still a little wary of it, but accepted her explanation. Jeremiah hopped down off the bathroom counter.

"Come on, baby," Mom said as she led him out.

Kia smiled at me when I looked back at her. She led the way out.

"I can't believe you're a 'mommy'," I commented. She put her hands in her pockets as we got to the living room.

"I can't believe it either sometimes." She sighed. "Actually, I kinda have to tell you something." I raised my eyebrows curiously. "You might need to sit down," she told me as she gestured at the couch.

Miss Anita walked in before she could get into it.

"Sorry to interrupt again," her mother said, "but we're about to eat."

We both nodded and she walked back out. I looked into Kia's eyes again.

"What were you sayin'?" I asked. She waved it off.

"Oh, it was nothin'."

I could tell by her expression that whatever it was, it was important. I was concerned.

"Are you sure?"

"Yeah, umm, we can talk about it another time."

Kia

I sighed as I watched David play basketball with J.D. and Bobby in the driveway later that evening. David picked J.D. up and helped him make a basket. Liyah came up beside me as I leaned on the deck railing.

"Those two seem to be getting along," she remarked.

"I know," I said sadly without looking at her.

"Chunky, you need to tell him."

"I know I do," I repeated. *I just don't know how.*

"Hey, whatchu thinkin' about?" Karen asked me.

We were at Chuck E. Cheese's. We'd brought J.D. and Karen's little boy, Gary, out as a treat. I'd zoned out watching my own little boy, wondering how the hell I was gonna tell David the truth.

"David," I told her honestly.

"Have you told him yet?" she asked, correctly reading my thoughts. David and I had spoken to each other over the phone every day for the past three weeks. We were playing catch up. Four years was the longest we'd ever gone without speaking or seeing one another.

I shook my head.

"I've been waiting for the right time," I told her.

"*Is* there a right time for something like this? Three

years of your son's life have already gone by without David knowing." I put my head in my hands.

"I know."

She stood up, abruptly ending our conversation. Gary had just fallen and hurt his arm, and Karen went to soothe his tears.

We went to the mall afterward. And wouldn't you know the boys were still hyper after all that playing. J.D. alone was trouble, but the both of them together was almost hell.

"Jeremiah!" I called as his hand slipped out of my grasp. I chased him, weaving in and out of passersby. "Jeremiah!"

Suddenly J.D. was lifted up by a strong pair of arms and I looked up with a smile.

"Where do you think you're going?" David was saying as J.D. squirmed and cried in his arms.

"Thank you," I said as he handed my son to me.

"No problem. He's an energetic little guy, isn't he?"

"You have no idea," I stated with a shake of my head and another grin. Karen caught up to us.

"You caught him, huh?" she asked me with a laugh. I nodded and put Jeremiah down, tightly holding onto his hand. She looked at David and smiled.

"Wassup, 'Ren?" he asked, smiling back.

"Nothin' much. You know, marriage, kids, the usual," she told him with a grin as she held up her engagement and wedding rings to show him.

"Congratulations," he said as he looked at the rings.

"Thanks." She looked at me. "Listen, I'm gonna go get the boys some dinner." She pointed at the food court.

"You sure you can handle both of them by yourself?" I asked in concern.

"Oh yeah, girl," she told me with a wave of her hand. "You stay here and talk to David." She held out her hand. "Come on, J.D." He looked up at both me and David before he obliged.

"I'll be over in a second, sweetie," I assured him.

They walked off and I looked into David's eyes again. I smiled.

"So, *BK*, you just go out without security now?" He shook his head with a big grin on his face.

"They're here." He pointed out one of his guys, a few steps behind him in a pair of jeans and a T-shirt. "I just don't like them to be all on my back. What about you, Kia Haughton? I don't see any security for you." I crossed my arms.

"When I'm with my son, people leave me alone for the most part."

"So, what's been up?" he asked. I shrugged.

"Nothin' really." I hesitated and thought about what 'Ren had said earlier. There really wasn't a right time to talk when dealing with certain things. "Actually, I kinda wanted to talk to you about somethin'."

His phone rang before he could reply. I sighed in relief, knowing that I wasn't ready to tell him anyway. He held up his index finger as he answered and chatted briefly.

"Sorry 'bout that," he said. "I almost forgot that I was meeting Kareem here. What did you wanna talk to me about?"

"Oh, umm, forget it. It wasn't that important." He raised his eyebrows.

"You sure? 'Cuz you're picking at your fingernails like you do when you get nervous."

I hadn't even realized. I smiled.

"You know me too well." He smiled back. "OK, J.D. is stayin' over Liyah's this weekend, and I wanted to know if you would come over." Actually, J.D. wasn't staying there, but I would be sure to make it happen. I think fast on my feet. David grinned.

"Aight. I'll be there." We hugged each other. "See you then."

I nodded as he walked off.

David

I called Kia to get her address that Saturday, and then

headed out. I looked around when I got to her neighborhood. She damn sure had come up from that condo she had a few years ago. The houses weren't mansions, but they were close—huge backyards, pools, and wraparound driveways. I drove up to her brick house, parked in her driveway, and walked up onto the front porch. I rang the bell and waited. No answer. I rang again. Still no answer.

I took out my cell and dialed hers.

"Hey," I said when she picked up. "I'm here. Where you at?"

"Oh, is it six o'clock already? I'm out back in the pool. I just wanted to go for a quick swim, but I guess I lost track of time," she told me. "Follow that path on the side of the house."

"OK," I said and clicked off. I walked around the side of the house to the back.

Kia was climbing out of the pool when I got there. I could feel an erection coming on as soon as I saw her. She had on this tiny, red bikini that really didn't leave much to the imagination. I noticed that her body hadn't changed much, even after having a baby. She was still all curves with no flaws. She grinned at me as she grabbed her towel off one of her lawn chairs. I grinned back.

"Goddamn, girl," I said, "if you're trying to entice me, you're doing a good job." I pulled her into my arms before she could respond. I wanted her right then, right there. It'd been four long years, and I couldn't wait any longer. I kissed her lips. I picked her up and put her on the table beside us. She started to breathe deeply as I kissed and licked her neck. I untied her top and pulled it off before I began massaging her breasts. She started to pull off my clothes, and then she pulled me inside her after I untied her bikini bottom. I kissed her deeply as I paused to savor the moment. I moaned and smiled when I felt her muscles squeezing my dick. She smiled back and then bit her bottom lip as I started to thrust.

We both moaned when I came. She gasped as I pulled out. I sat down in one of the chairs, spent. I picked up her bikini bottom and held it in front of her.

"So," I said, "you gon' tell me this shit wasn't planned?" She giggled and held up her hands in innocence.

"I swear." I chuckled.

"Yeah, right."

The phone in the house rang. She hopped up to get it.

"I'll be right back," she said as she ran into the house.

I smiled as I watched her ass, dimple and all, jiggle the entire way. I got up and put my boxers and jeans back on. Then I sat back down and surveyed my surroundings. I was reflecting on how far we'd come when Kia came back outside, still as naked as newborn baby. She walked over to the table, picking up a pair of shorts and a halter top.

"Wait," I said, grabbing her hand before she could get dressed. "I just wanna look at you." She smiled. I licked my lips and smiled back as I scanned her body. "Do you even realize how beautiful you are?" She giggled. "I'm serious." I pulled her closer to me. She straddled my lap and then I kissed her again, deeply.

"You are gonna get me started again if you keep kissing me like that," she told me with a grin. I called her bluff and kissed her again more, passionately than the last time. She stood and said, "Come on," as she grabbed my hand and led the way into the house.

I smiled to myself when I woke up beside her the next morning. We'd made love so many times the night before that there was no way I could feel more relaxed. She didn't even get to show me the house. I didn't even have the energy to go out and run. I looked at the clock on the nightstand. It was almost noon, but I decided to let her sleep anyway. I kissed her forehead and got up.

I put on my boxers and quickly ran outside to my car. I grabbed my bag out of the backseat and came back inside. I took a shower, brushed my teeth, and put on basketball shorts with a wife-beater. I decided to take a look around myself since I didn't get the chance last night. She had a beautiful house. The studio was my last stop. I was amazed when I got in there. It was huge, and all the equipment was brand new. I

smiled as I sat down in one of the chairs. I was proud of Kia.
She'd made a successful career out of all of her talents.

"Kia, you in there?" I heard a voice say, interrupting
my thoughts. I looked around and noticed security feeds
above me. Liyah was at the front door with Jeremiah. I
looked around again for the button to the intercom and found
it.

"Naw," I said, "she's still 'sleep," I told her sister.

"Still asleep?" she asked with a shake of her head.
Then she smiled. "Y'all musta had fun last night, huh." I
laughed and pushed the button again.

"I'll be there in a sec," was my only response.

I shut the door behind me and walked down the hall
toward the living room. I smiled as I opened the front door.
Liyah grinned back at me.

"I can't stay," she said. "I just came to drop off J.D."
She handed me his bag. "He hasn't eaten lunch yet," she told
me. I nodded as he walked inside. Liyah kissed my cheek.
"I'll see you later." I smiled.

"Yeah."

"Bye, J.D.," she said.

He walked back over to his aunt and hugged her. She
kissed his forehead and then was off. I shut the door and
looked down at Jeremiah.

"Aight, lil' man," I said. "Let's go put your stuff
away, and then I'll fix you somethin' to eat."

He headed to the stairs without a word, and I followed.

Kia

It was one-thirty and David had already gotten out of
bed when I woke up. I yawned and got up to brush my teeth.
I put my hair up into a ponytail and then went downstairs.
David was sitting on the couch eating a bowl of cereal with
J.D. and watching the Disney channel. I crossed my arms
and grinned at the sight.

I walked over to the couch, looked down at David,

and kissed his lips.

"Did you have a nice sleep?" he asked. I nodded.

I walked over to where J.D. was sitting and crouched down. I kissed his cheek. He smiled at me.

"Did you have fun at your Auntie Liyah's?" I asked.

"Yes," he replied. I kissed him again and stroked his head full of long, curly hair.

"You should lemme cut his hair," David stated as he put his bowl down on the coffee table. I giggled a little as I stood up.

"Oh no, that is not happenin'."

"Why not?" he asked, looking up at me curiously.

"Because, he won't even let *me* cut it. He screams bloody murder when I do take the clippers to his head, so I just let it grow out. I mean, it's only hair, right? As long as it's clean and combed, it's not that big of a deal." David smiled as he stood too.

"Betchu I could cut it with him quiet." I smirked.

"I gotta see that to believe it, babe." He grinned.

"Aight, then. Let's go upstairs and I'll show you how it's done." I laughed again.

"OK." I looked down at my son. "Come on, swee-tie."

Jeremiah followed David and I up the stairs to the bathroom. I'd just handed David the hair clippers when the phone rang.

"Oh shoot," I said. I smiled at David. "Don'tchu start without me." He just grinned at me.

I ran to my bedroom to grab the phone. It was my mother. We chatted briefly and then I walked back into the bathroom. To my complete and utter shock, David was cutting J.D.'s hair and J.D. was quietly sitting there on the toilet seat cover. My jaw dropped.

"How did you do that?" I asked David.

"I'll never tell," he told me with a big grin. "It's a guy thing. You wouldn't understand."

I giggled and that's when I noticed David's own head. He'd obviously cut his hair down low to show Jeremiah that there was nothing to be afraid of.

"Oh, I see," I said, gesturing at his haircut. He nodded.

"Like I said, a guy thing. You, a woman, wouldn't shave off your own hair, so he never knew that it was painless."

I nodded and leaned against the counter with my arms crossed, just watching. David cut J.D.'s hair and even gave him a shapeup. He put both sets of clippers down on the counter and came over to me.

"And that's how it's done," he stated with a smile.

"Thank you," I said, pulling him into me. He kissed my lips and we got lost in each other for a moment until J.D. started to push his way in between us. David and I started laughing.

"Looks like someone is jealous," David said. He looked down at our son with raised hands as he backed up. "Hey, man, it's OK. I'm not tryna steal your mommy. We can share, can't we?"

J.D. just looked up at him with wide eyes, still holding onto me. David chuckled.

"He's madd protective of you," he said to me.

"Well, yeah," I said, laughing myself. "He's been the lil' man of the house for three years. You're stepping on his toes a little."

David laughed again and my heart ached a bit. I knew I would have to tell him, *especially* if he and J.D. were starting to get used to each other.

The moment of truth came that evening. All three of us were in the living room. J.D. was passed out on the loveseat beside David and me. David had worn him out playing catch in the backyard. David and I sat on the couch watching a movie. He put his arm around me and kissed my lips, then looked into my eyes seriously when he pulled away.

"Can I ask you somethin'?" he asked. I nodded.

"Sure."

He glanced over at our son.

"Where's his father?" I sighed.

"He's . . . around. It's kinda complicated between me and his dad."

"Well, does J.D. get to see him?" I nodded. "Actually, they saw each other just recently." David raised his eyebrows and nodded. I exhaled again and told myself to just do it. I pulled away and looked into the eyes that he and J.D. shared.

"Listen," I started, but the phone rang. I couldn't say that I wasn't relieved, but it seemed like every time I got up the nerve to be honest, somethin' stopped me. I groaned and picked up the cordless beside me. "Hello," I said in a stressed tone.

"Hey, girl," Candice said on the other end. "You OK? I'm not interrupting anything, am I?"

"Well," I began and looked at David, "hold on a sec." I took the phone from my ear as I stood up. "I'll be right back, OK?"

"Alright," David said, smiling slightly.

I walked down the hall and into the studio, shutting the door behind me.

"Candice, I was just about to tell 'im," I said into the receiver as I sat down in one of my chairs.

"Who? David? You were gonna tell him about Jeremiah?" I nodded on my end.

"Yeah."

"Oh, I'm sorry. Get back to it."

"Too late," I said. "I already lost my nerve."

"Kia, you can't keep postponing this."

"I know, I know, I know. It's not that easy, alright?"

"Nobody said it would be easy, Chunky, but you can't keep running from every opportunity."

CHAPTER 14

David

"Wassup, man?" I asked Kareem at the airport a couple weeks later. We gave each other dap and hugged. "How you been, dawg?"

"Good. How are things out here?" he asked as we made our way over to baggage claim. But I knew he really meant what was up with me and Kia. I smiled.

"Really, really good actually." He looked at me.

"Yeah, you look madd happy," he said with grin. I nodded.

"Me and her son are even getting along."

He raised his eyebrows as he grabbed his suitcase and bag.

"Really?" I nodded. "I hate to rain on your parade, but what are you gonna do now? I mean, have you even talked to your wife?" I shook my head.

"I'm still torn about everything," I told him honestly. "Especially now that me and Kia have reconnected."

"Do you still love Chrissy, man?" I nodded again.

"Of course I do. Me and her have been through so much."

We headed out to my car. Kareem shook his head.

"You really need to make a decision. You can't keep getting closer to Kia *and* her son, dawg. That's just asking for trouble. Mark my words, Kia is gonna start to put pressure on you."

I popped the trunk and he put his luggage inside. Kareem always gave me a lot to think about. It was a quiet ride back to my mother's house.

Kia

"Oh shit," Karen said as we walked into the checkout line at Wal-Mart one Sunday.

"'*Ren*," I said firmly as I tried to cover our kids' ears. She looked down at all of them.

"Oh, sorry guys. Auntie 'Ren didn't mean it, honey," she said to my son. She grabbed a tabloid and showed it to me. "Have you seen this?" she asked.

The headline read "Rapper BK's Secret Love" and underneath was a picture of me and David kissing in front of my house. The pic was so clear that there was no denying it. Whoever took it was right across the street from my house when they shot it.

"Jesus," I said as I looked at it. "Ain't that a"—I glanced down at the kids—"B-I-T-C-H," I spelled out. I put the magazine down on the conveyor belt with the rest of our groceries with a sigh. It was only a matter of time before Christina caught wind of this.

I walked through Miss Pam's backdoor twenty minutes later. David was sitting at the kitchen table. I put the tabloid on the table in front of him without even a greeting.

"Have you seen this?" I started right in, sitting down across from him.

"What in the hell?" he said as he read the headline. He opened the magazine and looked at the other pictures. He then looked at me with a slight smile. "You know this is all your fault, right?" I furrowed my brow.

"How's that?"

"The paparazzi love you. You're the R&B superstar. If it had been me and someone else, it never would've made it to the press. They don't care about me. I'm just some rapper. You don't see Nas in no tabloids, do you?" I giggled.

"Shut up," I said, hitting him in the leg. "That's not true. You were in the tabloids a lot when you and wifey were havin' problems." He nodded.

"Yeah, but other than that, nothing."

"Don't make jokes, though. This is serious." David shrugged.

"What do you want me to say? There's nothing we can do about it now." Kareem walked into the kitchen just then.

"Yo, have you seen the *Enquirer*?" he asked.

David made a face at me and we both laughed from our spots at the table.

"Yes, we've seen it," David said.

"You know this is gonna bring a storm of questions, right? They ain't even gon' be focusing on the album now because of this shit."

"I'll just dodge them like I usually do, keep the focus on the music. It's not like there weren't questions about me and Kia before."

"You're awfully nonchalant about this."

"What am I s'posed to do, dawg? Sue the press for actually telling the truth for once? This ain't nothin'. I can handle the heat, trust me." Kareem raised his eyebrows.

"Oh? What about the heat that your wife'll bring when she comes out here?"

Good question, I thought. It also begged another question. What was gonna happen the next time David actually talked to her? Would I be put on the back-burner once again?

David looked at him seriously.

"I can handle Christina, too."

Kareem's phone rang as he shook his head. He looked the ID.

"Excuse me, I have to take this, y'all."

David looked into my eyes when Kareem left. I looked back with a worried expression.

"What's wrong?" he asked. I shook my head. "Come 'ere," he said, gesturing for me to sit on his lap. I obliged and he kissed my cheek as he wrapped his arms around my waist. "You worried about Chrissy confronting you again?"

"No. Well, yeah. But that's not my *big* concern."

"What's your big concern?"

"Well, what *is* gonna happen the next time you see her, David?"

He paused like he was searching for the right answer to my question.

"Listen, I know right now you're lookin' for some stability in your life, a man to be there for you, a hundred percent of the time." He squeezed me. "A father for your son." If only he knew how dead on he actually was. "But things are just sooo complicated right now. I don't know if I can give you whatchu need."

That statement hit me like a bag of bricks. He made me feel like I was just, *a mistress*. I swallowed and opened my mouth to speak, but Kareem walked back into the kitchen. I stood up before I started to cry.

"I have to go," I announced. He grabbed my hand as I picked up my purse. I looked back at him.

"You OK?" he asked.

I nodded, even though I was clearly agitated.

David

"Hello?" I said as I picked up my cell while in my car. It was a few days after Kia had shown me the picture in that magazine.

"David, sweetie?" my mother asked.

"What's up, Mom?"

"Umm, Christina's here." I huffed.

"When'd she get there?"

"Just got here. Hasn't been here more than fifteen minutes. She seems really angry, too." I figured as much.

"OK, Mom, thanks for the head's up. I'm on my way home now."

I got there in another ten minutes.

"Where is she?" I asked my mother as I walked into the kitchen.

"Upstairs in your room," she told me.

I nodded and walked up the stairs. She was sitting on

the bed when I got there. She had on jeans and a T-shirt, and her hair was pulled up out of her face. She looked better than the last time I'd seen her. After we lost the baby she was so depressed that she barely ate, and as a result, she'd lost a lot of weight. She'd been too thin, but now she looked like she was back to normal. I shut the door behind me and put my hands in my pockets.

"Hey," I said.

She nodded and pulled out the magazine.

"Wanna explain this?" she asked as she placed it on the bed.

"I think it's pretty self-explanatory." She smirked.

"I can't believe you," she said with shake of her head.

"You can't tell me that you didn't expect this." She stood and crossed her arms.

"Guess I was being naïve, 'cuz I didn't think you would do it to me again, David. Not after the way you abandoned me in New York." I glared at her.

"Hold on a second, Christina. No one abandoned you. If I recall correctly, you repeatedly pushed me away. I tried to be there for you, but you just weren't havin' it. You touched me what, once? Twice? In the span of six months."

"I was depressed, David!"

"And you just shut me out, Chrissy! What the fuck was I s'posed to do?" She looked at me venomously.

"You should've stayed with me. Now I gotta find out from some magazine that you just walked back into *her* arms?!"

There was silence for a moment and I actually felt bad. I walked over to her and tried to put my arms around her.

"Don't fuckin' touch me, David," she said. She shoved me hard off her. I looked at her in shock and nodded.

"Aight," I said as I glared at her. I grabbed one of my bags from underneath the bed. I opened up one of my dresser drawers and started throwing clothes into the bag.

"What are you doing?!" she shouted.

"What the fuck does it look like?!" I yelled back.

"Wait, Dave," she said as she sobbed and tugged on my arm. "Baby, don't go. I'm so sorry."

"Hell if I'ma stay here witchu," I said as I freed my arm from her grasp. "You remember this shit next time you accuse someone of abandoning you."

I left her in the room as she broke down and sat on the floor, bawling. My mother tried to stop me from leaving as I headed for the backdoor.

"Mom, please get out of my way."

"David, you can't run from every fight."

"That woman is impossible to talk to."

"So what are you gonna do, Dave? Run to Kia?" I looked down at the floor. "That's what started all the problems in the first place." I sighed.

"Listen, you tell my wife that when she is ready to talk to me like a civilized person, call me. 'Til then, I cannot be in the same house with her."

My mother exhaled and let me go.

I was halfway to Kia's house when I called her from my cell. I knew we didn't leave each other on the best of terms the last time we'd seen each other, but right now I needed her as my friend, not my girl.

"Hey, I need to chill at your place for a while," I told her.

"Lemme guess, Christina's in town, right?"

"Yeah, and I do not want to deal with her."

"So you just run to me?"

"I need you right now."

"Hmph. Yeah, only when it's convenient."

"Huh?"

"Nothing. Can you hold on for a minute? Liyah's on the other line."

"OK," I said slowly. I was confused about her comment. She came back a second later. "So can I stay?" I asked. She hesitated.

"What's gonna happen when wifey finds my address and comes up here looking for you? I won't have Jeremiah exposed to her madness."

"Don't worry about that. She won't try anything if I'm there."

"Right." She paused. "I'm sorry, David, but I'm gonna have to say no."

"What?"

"I said, no." I pulled up in front of her house and parked across the street.

"Why not?"

"Because I can't do this anymore. You said yourself that you can't give me what I need, and you're right. I'm tired of being your backup plan." She walked out onto her front porch and looked at my car. "I just can't. I'm sorry, baby."

I clicked off. I looked into her eyes from my seat. I realized that my friend was gone. Too much had gone down between us for it to just go back to the way it was. She wanted all of me, but I couldn't give her that right now and she was fed up. I couldn't say that I really blamed her. I came to the realization that maybe I'd messed things up way too much with *both* of my women. I was glad Kia couldn't see me through my tinted windows. She wouldn't be able to see the pain in my eyes. I put the car in drive and sped off toward the freeway.

Kia

"I never thought I would see this day," Liyah commented. I'd just gotten through explaining to her what David had said the last time we saw each other.

"What day?" I asked as I finished making a PB&J sandwich for J.D. "Here you go, sweetie," I said to him as I placed it on the kitchen table.

"The day when you guys would switch roles. He becomes the player and you're the most faithful I think I've ever seen you."

I laughed as I sat down across from my son.

"I know, right?" My phone beeped and I took it away from my ear for a second to check the ID. "Goddamn," I said, using one of David's favorite words as his cell number flashed across the screen.

"What?" Liyah asked when I put the phone back to my ear. I smirked.

"That's 'the player' now. Hold on a sec, OK?"

"Alright."

I clicked over and David told me he wanted to stay at my place for a while. Of course, that was only because Christina was in town. I sighed, knowing him, he was probably already on his way over.

"Can you hold on for a minute?" I asked him. "Liyah's on the other line."

"OK," he said slowly. I clicked back over.

"Hey, I'm gonna have to call you back," I told my sister in a stressed tone.

"Is everything OK? You sound really agitated all of a sudden."

"Oh, I am. But I'm about to straighten his ass out right now. I'll call you right back."

"Alright."

I clicked over again.

"Still there?" I asked.

"Yeah. So can I stay?"

After I told him no because I knew in my heart that I just couldn't have only part of him anymore, I walked out onto my front porch and saw his car sitting across the street. "I just can't, I'm sorry, baby," I told him unhappily.

He hung up on me and I couldn't see him, but I knew he was looking at me through the darks tints of his windows. He drove off a second later.

I awoke from a deep sleep to the phone ringing a few nights later. I groaned and reached over to grab it.

"Hello?" I mumbled.

"I'm sorry. Did I wake you?" a male voice responded on the other end. I was cranky as hell.

"What do you think?" I was still groggy and didn't recognize the voice either. "Who is this?" The caller got smart right back.

"Who do you think it is? You expecting someone else this early?" I knew it could only be one person. No other guy would be so bold with me. I sat up and looked at the clock.

"David, why are you calling me at three in the morning?" I asked, ignoring his comment.

"Because I can't sleep and you're usually up late." I smiled and lay back down.

"Well, that was about three years and a baby ago." He laughed a little.

"You gotta keep up with the rugrat, huh?"

"Yeah." He paused.

"Baby, I'm sorry."

"For what?"

"For everything. I haven't been treatin' you right."

I sighed. I could never stay mad at him.

"I know, but you don't have to apologize."

"Yes, I do. I don't know how you've been so patient with me."

"Well, who understands the life of a pimp better than me?" He chuckled again.

"True dat. Can I come see you?"

I thought about it. I *did* want to see him. As fed up as I was with the situation between us, it didn't stop that need. I had such a weakness for this man.

"OK," I said. "I'll leave the backdoor open for you."

"Be there in like twenty minutes."

CHAPTER 15

Kia

"Can I have some juice?" my son asked me. It was a couple of weeks later. David and I were on speaking terms, but I still had not allowed him to stay with me. There had to be a line drawn somewhere, at least until he figured everything out.

"Can I have some juice....what?" I asked J.D., waiting for the magic word. He thought for a moment.

"Pleeeeaase," he answered with a big grin on his face. I giggled.

"Come on." I led the way to kitchen and opened the refrigerator. I grabbed the bottle of cranberry juice and then picked up one of his sippy cups from the sink. I opened up the bottle just as the phone rang. I looked over at where the phone was s'posed to be in the kitchen. It wasn't there. That's when I remembered that I'd been on the cordless talking to Liyah that morning. I looked down at J.D.

"Don't touch that," I said firmly, pointing at the bottle of juice. "I'll be right back."

I rushed into the living room to pick up the phone before the voice mail came on.

"Hello?"

"Hey, girl," I heard Candice's voice say. "What's goin' on?"

I sighed as I walked back over to the entryway of my kitchen.

"Nothin'. I'm just here tryna keep up with Jeremiah.

And, girl, is he ever bad."

"Had you runnin' around all day?" I turned away from my son for a moment.

"You don't know the half."

"Yeah, boys tend to be a lot more hyper than girls."

"God, you ain't never lied. Sometimes I think he's trying to get back at me for leaving him so much." I heard a bouncing, splooshing kind of sound and gasped as I turned back around to look at where J.D. had been standing. The bottle of cranberry juice that had been on the counter was now spilled all over the floor, and he was drenched in the red liquid from head-to-toe. He took off when I glared at him. "Candice, I'ma have to call you back." She giggled.

"Good luck."

I hung up and put the phone on the counter. I quickly wiped up the majority of the juice and went off to find him. He had tracked red juice all over my blue carpet.

"Jeremiah?!" I called. There was silence. "Boy, you better get your butt out here! I'm not playin' wit' you!" He crawled out from his hiding spot behind the living room couch. "Get over here right now," I said sternly. He hesitated with tears in his eyes. I narrowed my eyes at him, though, and stood my ground. "What'd I just say?" He came over to me then and I spanked his bottom, only once, but it got my point across. He started to cry harder. "*Enough* with all your mischief today."

"OK, M-M-Mommy," he stuttered as he looked up at me through tears. I knelt down to take off his wet clothing.

"Don't move," I told him as he stood there in his underwear, "I'm just going to put these in the laundry room."

He sniffed and wiped his eyes as I walked a few yards away and dropped the clothes on top of the washing machine. I walked back out and grabbed his hand.

"Come on," I said as I led him to the stairwell, "let's go put you in the tub, again."

He was quiet as I ran the water and filled the bathtub. And he didn't utter a word to me as I put him in the water. He didn't even splash around or play with his toys like he usually did. It made me feel awful. It *was* partly my fault. I was the one who left the open bottle on the counter. *Maybe I was too hard on him,* I thought. When I lifted him up outta the bath and dried him off, he looked into my eyes.

"Mommy?"

"Yes, sweetie?" I answered.

"Sorry," he said. His big, chocolate brown eyes were filled with sincerity.

I smiled. How could I stay mad at that face?

"Mommy's sorry too, baby, but you have to learn to listen, OK?" He nodded.

"OK." I wrapped my arms around him and kissed his forehead as he hugged me back.

We walked out of the bathroom and into his bedroom. Just as I put another pair of briefs and a mini wifebeater on him, the doorbell rang.

"Now who could that be?" I asked myself. I looked at the clock on his dresser—one o'clock. The only person I could think of that would just drop by would be David. There was only one way to find out. "Come on, baby, let's go see who it is," I said. J.D. followed me down the stairwell.

The doorbell rang again as we got to the bottom of the stairs.

"I'm comin', I'm comin'," I muttered. I opened the front door.

Christina stood there on my front porch with her arms crossed. Her dark hair fell past her shoulders and she was decked out in designer jeans, a white halter top that ruffled down past her hips, and her jewelry was all platinum and diamonds. Other than that, she looked exactly the same. But once again, she was a contrast to me in my juice-stained, once white T-shirt and sweatpants.

"Geez," was the only thing I managed to articulate. I looked at my son beside me. She looked at him too and then zeroed in on his arm. She looked at me and scoffed. *Oh shit,* I thought. *She noticed his birthmark.*

David had a birthmark on his right arm, shaped sort of like a tomahawk. His mother had the exact same one on her arm. It was hereditary, so naturally my son had the same mark on the same arm. And leave it to Christina to catch me out before I could tell David the truth.

I sighed and crouched down to look into J.D.'s face.

"Honey," I said, "can you be a good boy and go watch TV in the living room, please?" He nodded and ran off.

I opened up the screen door and joined my adversary on the porch. She crossed her arms.

"So, you were able to give him what I couldn't, huh?" I came to realize what she was gettin' at and did not respond. "I suppose you just couldn't wait to tell him either." I shook my head.

"It's not like that. He doesn't even know."

"He doesn't know?" she asked in surprise. I shook my head again. "He's gonna be sooo pissed at you when he finds out," she told me with a sort of laugh.

"How the hell did you figure out where I lived?" I snapped, abruptly changing the subject.

"David keeps an address book. He has for a while now. That's how I knew where you lived the first time, too."

"So, what? You came over here to beat me down in front of my son?"

"This is the second time I've found out about you and David. Oh, we were definitely gonna have words," she told me boldly. "But now, I don't know what to do."

"What are you talkin' about?"

"You win."

She caught me off guard with that and confused the shit outta me.

"What? Why?"

"'Cuz you have something that I don't. You have his son, and I"—she shrugged—"can't compete with that."

"So, that's all this has been to you? A competition?"

"You can't just take your victory and shut up, can you?" she asked, biting my head off.

I glared at her but shut my mouth. I was not about to start scrappin' with my little boy inside.

"If you don't mind," I said sharply, "I got things to do,

so . . ." I gestured inside.

She nodded and I watched as she walked down the steps and toward her car.

After I cleaned up J.D.'s mess, I got him settled watching a movie and then sat on the stairwell with the phone. I dialed my father's number. I was stressed out over David and I needed his advice.

"Hey, baby girl," I heard his deep voice say.

"Hi, Daddy," I replied.

"How's my grandson doing?"

"He's as bad as ever." Daddy chuckled.

"Keeps you on your toes." I laughed too.

"I guess."

"So what's goin' on?" he asked.

"I just need your words of wisdom right now."

"OK, whatchu wanna know?" I hesitated.

"Umm, what are your opinions about cheating?" He paused.

"Did your momma tell you to ask me that?" I giggled.

"No."

"Is this about David?" I sighed.

"Geez, did everyone know about me and him?"

"Your mother keeps me pretty updated about what's goin' on with my girls."

Figures, I thought.

"Did she tell you about J.D. too?"

"Not exactly. I kind of figured that out on my own and then she confirmed it. He has David's eyes." I exhaled again.

"I know."

"But he doesn't know, right?"

"Who, David or Jeremiah?"

"Both."

"No, neither of them knows. I don't know how to tell them, especially David. I'm just confused about everything. That's why I needed to call you."

"Well, let's get back to the cheating issue. As you

probably know by now, I did cheat on your mother when you and Liyah were little. Honestly, I think I've been on every side of cheating and I feel like it's a bad situation no matter how you try to spin it. Someone is always the loser."

"I know."

"Why are you involved with him if you feel that way?"

"Because I love him."

"We all do, sweetie. He's like a son to me, you know that, but you're my baby girl and I don't like to see you hurting."

"But when we're together, it doesn't hurt, Daddy. Everything is so right."

"Until he leaves again and then you're left to pick up the pieces of a broken heart."

"Yeah."

"Look, Chunky, I'm not telling you this to get you down, but you called to get the truth, right?" I nodded on my end.

"Yes, of course. That's why I called you. Everyone else is saying just hold on and wait, and if I just wait, he'll see that I'm the one he's s'posed to be with."

"Well, the way I see it is, you need to put your foot down. Since when do you let any man treat you like second best? That's not the strong woman that I raised, and you know it. I think it's time for you to give him an ultimatum. Make him choose—his wife or you. Otherwise, you three will just stay in this cycle."

"I was afraid you were gonna say that."

"Are you positive that he feels the same way about you that you feel about him?"

"Yes."

"Then there should be a positive outcome. If his back is put up against the wall, then he will definitely choose you."

"You're right. You're absolutely right," I said. "All this drama has gone on for far too long."

"So when are you gonna talk to him?"

"Tonight. I'm gonna call him as soon as I get off the

phone with you."

"Good. And if for some reason things don't go your way, then it's his loss."

I smiled. Talking to Daddy always made me feel better.

"Thank you for talking some sense into me."

"That's what I'm here for. One more thing, no matter what happens after your talk, make sure that you do tell him about Jeremiah. He deserves to know."

"OK, Daddy," I replied. "I will."

"I'm gonna go so you can make that phone call. I love you."

"I love, too. Bye."

I clicked off and looked at my son, still quiet and into the movie. I dialed David's number.

"Hello?" I heard him say after three rings.

"Hey, we need to talk," I told him.

"I agree," he said in a stressed tone.

"Can you come over?"

"Yeah, but not 'til like after ten. Is that alright?"

"Uh-huh. Don't ring the bell, though. Just knock, OK?"

"Alright."

David

"Alright y'all!" my photographer yelled. "That's a wrap!"

We all cheered and clapped. I had just finished up a shoot for *XXL* magazine and I was so happy. It'd been a long ass day. I couldn't stand photo shoots. They just took forever. But it went with the job.

I walked off the set and over to my dressing room. I closed the door and took off the shirt and wife-beater that I was wearing. I sat down in one of the chairs and put my head in my hands, trying to regroup. I was getting the worst migraine. But I was in my dressing room less than five minutes before someone was knocking on my door. I exhaled.

"What?" I called through the door. It opened and Christina poked her head inside.

I huffed again, I wasn't in the mood to fight. That was why I'd left New York in the first place. That was why I'd left her at my mother's house.

"What're you doing here?" I asked flatly.

"Damn," she said as she walked in without an invite and closed the door behind her. She sensed my aggravation. "What's with you?"

"I'm tired and I have a headache," I explained simply as I rubbed my temples and turned away.

"Have you eaten at all today?" I didn't answer, 'cuz I hadn't. "I've told you about going all day without eating, David." I looked at her through the mirror in front of me.

"Did you come here to lecture me about my eating habits or was there something else?" I asked so she'd get to the point.

"OK," she said, "so much for small talk. I came here to tell you that I want a divorce."

There was silence as I tried to process what she'd just said. Here I was, battling myself over this issue, and she made the decision without really putting much thought into it.

"Just like that?" I asked as I turned to look at her. "We haven't even been separated for three months." She shrugged.

"Yes, David, it's only been three months and already you're back with Kia." I glared at her.

"Yo, I am really sick and tired of you blamin' our problems on her!"

"Our problems started with her!"

"I made a mistake. I'm sorry. How many times can I say that shit?!" I shook my head. I couldn't believe that after all this time, Chrissy and I were right back to where we had started. I paused to calm myself. "Look, this is neither the time nor the place for this shit. Lemme change and I will meet you at my mother's house, aight?"

"Fine, but do *not* run away from this," she told me and then walked out.

I got up and changed out of jeans and into sweats.

Then I grabbed my car keys and walked outside. I got behind the wheel of my BMW and sped off.

Christina didn't waste any time when I got to Mom's house.

"I can't believe you're fuckin' her again," she said when I walked into our room.

"I needed to get it from somewhere, Chris," I shot back. Her eyes shot daggers at me.

"Fuck you."

"Exactly my point. You wouldn't, and that's why we're here."

"Don't you try to blame this on me! We *were* having sex when you cheated the first time!"

"OK! Goddamn! I made a mistake! And all I've done is try to make up for it since! I was the most devoted husband to you, but you were too blind to see it because you never gave me the benefit of the doubt."

"I gave you the benefit when you came out here, only to find out that you were steppin' out on me again."

"We're separated! You act like I just banged the first bitch I saw!" A tear fell from her eye.

"The fact that you have feelings for this *particular* bitch makes it worse than everything else. What is so great about her?!" I didn't respond. "And to think thatchu were fucking her without protection."

I looked into her eyes. She'd never questioned me on that before.

"What the fuck are you talkin' about?" I asked suspiciously.

"Wouldn't you like to know," she said in a childish manner. I frowned at her.

"Christina, I'm not in the mood for games, OK? How do you know that I wasn't using protection?" She hesitated.

"Why don't you ask your beloved Kia?"

"Ask her what? You know somethin' I don't?" She shrugged and that just made me more agitated. "Spit it out," I said firmly.

"Aight," she said nonchalantly. "You have a son."

I looked at her like she'd gone insane.

"What?"

"Kia's little boy, he's your son." I smirked.

"You're lying."

"No, I'm not."

"*Yes*, you are. You think Kia wouldn't have told me had she been pregnant with *my* child? You think her mother or mine wouldn't have said anything? You're crazy."

"Oh, am I? He has the same birthmark as you and your mom. I saw it with my own two eyes."

"You saw? When?"

"I was at Kia's house earlier today," she admitted, actually looking kind of ashamed. I shook my head.

"Unbelievable. What the hell were you doing at her house? How did you even know where she lived?"

"None of that matters. What's important is what I found out when I went over there. She admitted it to me and everything, I swear."

I looked into her eyes and she looked straight into mine.

"You're serious, aren't you."

"Why would I make up something like this?" I didn't answer. She looked at me sadly. "Listen, I'm telling you this because I think you need to know, and not to put her in a bad light, although what she did is pretty dirty. I know nothing will steer you away from her anyway. If anything, this will probably just bring you two closer." I still said nothing. I started to piece things together in my mind. Things finally made sense. I was still trying to cope with what I'd just heard when my cell phone rang.

I unclipped it from my pants and looked at the ID. Kia. *Perfect mothafuckin' timing*, I thought. I flipped the phone open and clicked on. She said we needed to talk, and I agreed to go to her house over later that night.

I hung up and looked at my wife, who was leaning against the bedroom doorway.

"Look, *I'm* gonna sleep in a hotel tonight," Chrissy said. "We can, uh, discuss lawyers and paperwork and everything tomorrow."

I nodded and she walked out.

I arrived at Kia's at five after ten and knocked on the front door. She came to the door a moment later, lookin' like she'd just woken up. She gestured for me to come inside, then she locked the door behind me. It was dark inside the living room other than the soft glow of the TV. She put a finger to her lips and motioned toward her sleeping son on the couch. Or I should say, *our* sleeping son. So many feelings ran through me as I thought about that.

"Come on," she said quietly. She grabbed my hand and led me to the kitchen. She turned on the lights and faced me as I rubbed my temples. "You still get those awful migraines?" I nodded. They had been a problem for a while. "Did you eat anything today?" I shook my head. "I got some leftover Chinese in the fridge. Want some?" I nodded again and then she took the food out of the refrigerator. She scooped me out a plate and heated it up. When it was done, she handed it to me and we sat at the kitchen table.

"What did you want to talk to me about?" I asked after I'd eaten a couple of mouthfuls.

"Wifey stopped by here earlier." I rolled my eyes.

"I heard."

"I did not appreciate it, David. This shit is getting a little ridiculous. We are in the exact same position we were in four years ago. And I'm getting a little tired of it. I don't play second fiddle to nobody, feel me?" I nodded. "You need to get your shit together, for real."

"Oh, it's that simple, right? Get my shit together. I swear, the both of y'all are driving me nuts with all your demands."

"Hey, I never asked anything of you. I told you to be with *her*, remember?"

"Yeah, *you* told me to be with her, and now you're makin' me choose."

"I've tried to be understanding about this, but this shit ain't fair to me."

I pushed my food away and scowled at her, angry now.

"You wanna talk about fair? Was it fair for you to keep the fact you gave birth to *my* son a secret?" She hesitated in responding at first. I read her expression and immediately knew it was true. Kia looked at me solemnly.

"She told you?" she asked.

"Yes, she told me. Now whatchu got to say about it?"

"I didn't know how to tell you. And under the circumstances—"

"It just slipped your mind?"

"No. I didn't want to bring my son up in that environment."

"Didn't I have a say about what type of environment *our* son would be brought up in?"

"David, I was not gonna raise him amidst all the drama that was goin' down."

"You know I would've left her in a heartbeat had I known."

"And that would've ended well considering her temper," Kia said sarcastically.

"I asked you about his father. You lied to my face." She looked down at her hands.

"What was I s'posed to say?"

"You could've told me the truth." There was silence for a moment. "He's gone three years without his dad," I commented.

"J.D. has never wanted for anything."

"Jeremiah David, right?" I correctly guessed. She didn't respond. "A woman cannot raise a man, Kia."

"Excuse me, but I think I'm doin' a damn good job. And your mother did perfectly alright with you, didn't she?"

"Yeah, she did everything she could. But a man will never truly be whole without his father." I shook my head and looked into her eyes. "You should've told me, especially because of the fact that I grew up without my dad. I wouldn't wish that on anyone."

There was another silence and then she grabbed my

hand.

"Baby, I'm sorry. You're absolutely right. I should've told you everything, but I just did what I thought was best at the time."

"Who else knew?" I asked. She sighed.

"Just about everyone." I shook my head again.

"My own mother lied to me," I remarked.

"Don't be mad at her," Kia told me. "I didn't want her to tell. She was just respecting my wishes. Besides, it was my responsibility to tell you, not hers."

"Right." I would be sure to talk to Mom about that later. I thought of something. "I thought you were on birth control that night," I said.

"I was."

"OK, so what happened? I thought that shit was s'posed to be like ninety-nine percent effective or something."

"Yeah, but there is so much room for error with things like that. I probably was off on my timing when I took it or something. Or maybe I'm just that rare one percent. I don't know."

"So you were pregnant during the wedding?" She nodded.

"About six months."

"What about the last time we had sex? How do we know you're not pregnant right now?"

"I had my period last week. Besides, I changed to a different prescription after the last time."

I nodded and then sighed. I couldn't even express the sadness that I was feeling. I'd been robbed of everything— finding out she was pregnant, watching her belly grow for nine months, being in the delivery room, J.D.'s first steps, his first words, all of it. I guess my sorrow showed when I looked back into her eyes, because she quickly apologized.

"I'm so sorry. I wanted to tell you sooner. I tried to, but I just didn't know how. And as time went on it became so much more difficult . . . I just . . ." She exhaled and her eyes began to well up.

I tugged on her hand and pulled her over to me. She

straddled me and we embraced each other. I kissed the tears off her cheeks.

"I'm sorry, too," I told her.

"For what?"

"For everything. It should've been me and you from the start, but I wasn't man enough to say it." I paused. "She told me that she wants a divorce," I said. Kia looked at me in surprise.

"How do you feel about that?" she asked. I shrugged.

"I don't know how to feel about it. I mean, I did love her, but it was nowhere near what I feel for you."

"Yeah, but she was still your wife." I thought about that.

"I almost feel . . . relieved." I looked into Kia's eyes with a slight smile. "Is that wrong?" She shook her head.

"Considering all the stress that went along with dealing with that woman?" She smiled. "No, I don't think that's wrong at all." She kissed my lips. "But then again, I do have a biased opinion." I laughed a little.

"So, what happens now?"

"I guess you get to know your son. I mean, better than you have." I nodded and she laughed. "Dealing with him on an everyday basis won't be an easy task, trust me."

"Why you say that?" I asked curiously.

"That boy is just bad." I laughed.

"Really?" She nodded.

"I don't know where he got that mischievous streak from, but he can be a handful. Like today I left an open bottle of cranberry juice on the counter and specifically told him not to touch it when I went to grab the phone from the next room. You know I had my back turned not thirty seconds before that juice was everywhere?" I cracked up.

"You serious?" I looked at her stained T-shirt. "Oh, is that what happened to you? I was gonna ask." She laughed again.

"Yes. David, the boy was soaked from head to toe, and then he ran into the living room and tracked it all over the carpet." She got up and grabbed my hand. She led me to the entryway and pointed. "All the way over to the couch. I was heated."

"What'd you do?"

"Spanked his little butt, put him in the tub, and then spent the majority of the day cleaning the kitchen, mopping the floor, and scrubbing the rug. That boy is too much, I'm telling you." We both started laughing again, but stopped when we heard J.D. squirming from the couch. Kia started toward it, but I stopped her.

"May I?" She looked up at me and smiled.

"Sure."

He looked up at me with wide eyes when I walked around the couch.

"Wassup, boy?" I asked as I picked him up. He shocked me by not crying or anything. He just put his head on my shoulder and started to fall back asleep. I smiled at him and then at Kia from across the room. She grinned as I headed for the stairs.

"Yes, he has his sweet moments," she said quietly. She stood up on her tiptoes, stroked his curly hair, and kissed his forehead. "Mommy's sweet baby."

We both walked upstairs then and put him to bed. She put on the baby monitor and we walked out into the hall. She looked up in my eyes.

"You stayin' the night?" she asked and I nodded. I slid my arms around her as we walked over to the next room and I kissed her neck.

I took off my shirt as she went over to her dresser. I took off my pants and she changed into biker shorts and a tank top. She looked at me seriously when she turned around.

"What," I said.

"Can I ask you somethin'?" I smiled.

"I think we know each other a little too well to be offended by personal questions." She smiled back. "Shoot."

"When Christina was here, and she saw J.D.'s birth-mark and everything, she said that I was giving you something that she couldn't. What did she mean by that?" I looked at her seriously then.

"We had a miscarriage a before I came out here." I looked down. "It was really hard on both of us. We wanted to try again, but the doctors said it was too risky. Her body for some reason just wouldn't be able to carry a baby for the entire nine months." I looked back into Kia's eyes. "And that's when things *really* started to go downhill." I shrugged.

Nothing was said after that. She nodded and we got into bed. I slipped my arms around her when she turned her back to me. She drifted off quickly while I lay there and thought about things. I was holding the mother of my child in my arms. The gravity of that overwhelmed me. And I think it made me fall deeper in love with her in just one night, like before. It made me happy, but it also made me very sad, because it meant Christina was right. The fact that I knew about Jeremiah had brought me closer to Kia. I would never feel that with Chrissy, so there was no turning back. My marriage was over. And a new life was finally just beginning.

Kia

I awoke later that night to the sound of thunder and lightning outside my window. I propped myself up on my elbow and listened to the baby monitor. David opened his eyes.

"What's wrong?" he asked. I put my right index finger on his lips and pointed at my ear with the other one. We heard the pitter-patter of tiny footsteps running toward our bedroom door a second later and I smiled.

J.D. popped his head into the room.

"Hey, lil' man," I said.

"How'd you know he was gonna do that?" David asked. I smiled again and pointed at the window.

"He's afraid of the thunder."

David smiled too and J.D. walked over to my bedside.

"You wanna sleep with us?" I asked him. He nodded, but hesitated because of David. "It's alright, baby. There's room." I patted a spot in the middle of us. "Come on."

He climbed up and got under the covers. He drifted off in a matter of moments. David looked into my eyes from across the bed. I smiled at him and touched our son beside me. David slid his hand into mine, fingers intertwining our fingers, and he started to fall back to sleep as well. I smiled again. Yeah, I could definitely do this for the rest of my life.

Epilogue

Kia

So, eight months have passed and things couldn't be better between me and David. To our surprise, Christina signed the divorce papers without any problems. She was so civil about it that it almost made me nervous. But at the same time, I was glad that I wouldn't have to deal with her any longer. David, J.D., and I became a real family then. David moved into the house with us and the two of them became really close. Jeremiah even started to call him Dad. And then we found out that I was expecting again, and our second little boy should be here in three months. Looked like I didn't have choice about pushing back the third album back now, huh.

I walked into my favorite soul food restaurant one Friday night. Me and David were gonna have a date night. Karen had agreed to watch J.D. while we spent some time alone together. The hostess smiled at me.

"Who's your party?" she asked.

"Green, please," I said.

"Right this way," she said as she grabbed two menus.

I looked around curiously at the empty restaurant and looked at my watch. It was nine-thirty in the evening. This place should've been packed. It also looked like someone went overboard with Valentine's Day decorations. White hearts and streamers were put up everywhere. *What the hell is going on here?* I wondered.

David came out from a backroom then. He had on a blue, button-down shirt and black dress pants. I smiled at him.

"Hi, baby," I said. "What is all this?"

He smiled back and then got down on one knee, pulling out a velvet box. He opened it up without a word. I was looking down at a huge pink diamond in a platinum setting.

Who knew how many carats it had? I immediately started to cry.

"Oh my god," I said as I placed my right hand over my chest. He grabbed my left hand and placed the ring on it, kissing it gently.

"Listen," he began, "I feel like my whole life has been leading up to this very moment. It's destiny, baby. Will you marry me right here, right now?"

I looked down at him in shock.

"What? Now? I'm not even dressed." I thought it was gonna be a regular night so I just had on jeans and a tank top.

"You're still the sexiest pregnant woman in the world. Who cares about what you're wearing. Just say you will." I giggled and then thought as I wiped my eyes.

"Our mothers are going to kill us. You know that, right?" He stood up with a chuckle.

"Is that a yes?" I nodded.

"Yes."

He kissed my lips and embraced me. That's when everyone came out of the backroom cheering. Momma, Liyah, and Daddy, Candice, Jaynie, 'Ren, Miss Pam, Kareem, Robert, Candice's husband, Jared, and Karen's husband, Jeff were all there. Our little boy was there with all the kids. And of course, there was a priest.

"Oh my god," I said again. And then I really started bawling. David had set everything up perfectly. He knew I would want the entire family there to witness our wedding.

I hugged and kissed everyone.

"Shall we get started?" the priest asked.

I looked up at my soon-to-be husband and we both nodded.

We held hands in the middle of the room as our loved ones surrounded us. David wiped the tears that rolled down my cheeks as he smiled at me.

"Dearly beloved, we are gathered here today . . ."

Moreover . . .

Christina

Oh, you guys thought I was gonna letchu leave without gettin' the last word in, huh? Well I got a few things I would like to say. First off, I am not crazy, not unless you count being crazy in love. Yeah, so what I fucked up that bitch's car? I would do it again in a heartbeat. Like I said, I loved that man, but I did not like being fucked with. And he is gonna get his, that's for damn sure.

The doctors said I wouldn't be able to carry a baby to full term, but they were wrong as usual. I stopped taking my birth control after the miscarriage, because I didn't see the point, but then I got pregnant. Yeah, I was pregnant with a baby girl when I divorced David. Why didn't I tell him? 'Cuz payback is a bitch. You didn't think I was gonna let him get off that easy, did you? I'm gonna bring him to court for child support and take him for all he's got. It'll be easy street for me. I paid my dues dealin' with all this cheatin' bullshit, and I deserve anything I can get.

"Waaaaahhhh!"

Oh shoot, that's my little bundle of joy now. The demands of motherhood are never-ending.

Butchu be sure to heed my words. It *ain't* over. It ain't over by a long shot . . .